The Retreat

Anne Pelling

To Heather
I hope you enjoy the
Retreat + thank you
for supporting it!
Anne Pelling

SpellBound Books

First Published by in 2025 by SpellBound Books

Chapter 1

Saturday 5th August 2023

Erica Mills was tearing along in the fast lane of the M5. Her speedo clocked she had managed to coax her elderly Corsa up to eighty-five miles per hour without too much effort and she flew passed the Asda lorry. It had been hogging the centre lane for the last mile. As she darted across in front of the offending juggernaut, she proceeded to indicate her intentions to continue across to the slow lane which was blatantly devoid of vehicles. It really was a pet peeve of hers when other drivers thought it was below them to set foot (or should that be tyres) in the *'slow'* lane. The Sat Nav interrupted her thoughts to remind her there was a speed camera in the vicinity, so easing her foot off the gas, she engaged the cruise control until all danger had passed. Erica was all too conscious of the pitfalls of speeding having experienced the joys of a Speed Awareness course. She preferred not to repeat the experience.

What was it the smug course leader, Nick, had said, she asked herself. In a mocking voice, she recalled aloud his wise recommendation. "Leave five minutes earlier rather than speed."

Responding, 'if I left five minutes early, I would just arrive five minutes early!' had not been her brightest move. Nick's scowl had conveyed to all that he was not too impressed. He had quietly reminded everyone present that it was in their best interest to take the course seriously if they wanted to leave without points being added to their licences. Erica had muttered an apology and resolved to keep quiet.

Chapter 2

Wednesday 6th November 2019

Travelling from her home to Bristol in the rush hour was never straight forward. There had been a hard frost. She had been grateful for her heated windscreen which saved her valuable minutes by rapidly tackling the ice. She had been confident of arriving at the Speed Awareness centre in good time having allowed an hour and a half to travel. The A4 into Bristol was a minefield of speed, red light, and bus lane cameras which she had negotiated successfully on many occasions. She was on high alert as she made her way into the city. The traffic was building as she passed the familiar grand Victorian façade of Bristol Temple Meads Railway station. The clock in the centre of the ornate stonework informed her that it was eight forty-five as she finally ground to a halt. By her reckoning she was only ten minutes away from her final destination, but the clock was ticking down fast. Cursing the roadworks, she finally pulled into the car park with five minutes to spare. She grabbed her rucksack and, after taking a quick photo of *'Carla the Karma Llama'* for the class scrap book, flew through the entrance. She narrowly missed barging into the sign directing her to the appropriate room for her course. Rushing through the doors she scanned the room for a seat near the back and collapsed into it, dropping her bag on the floor. She was not in the mood to participate and hoped to keep herself to herself.

As the course leader made his introduction and welcomed everyone, Erica hoped she didn't look too hot and flustered. She was still chuntering to herself about the traffic and worrying about her appearance when Nick held up a familiar object which he had picked up on the way through the door. It was *'Carla the Karma Llama'* who must have fallen out of her rucksack as she rushed in. She felt her face flush and burn as she tentatively raised her hand to acknowledge ownership of the toy. There was not enough time for her to explain the purpose of Carla as her *'classroom therapy pet,'* so she quietly retrieved the toy and returned it to the rucksack beneath the table.

Nick brought the class to his attention and continued the course. "It's a good idea to leave five minutes earlier rather than risk speeding," he suggested.

Still rattled by the humiliation of Carla, Erica found herself answering back. "If I left five minutes earlier, I would probably arrive five minutes earlier," she muttered. She heard other *'victims'* murmuring and chuckling in appreciation of her bravery. The look on Nick's face told a different story. No wonder I reacted, she justified to herself, as she shuffled in her seat.

She soon christened Nicholas Ryder, *'Annoying Nick'* as he had irritated her from the beginning. It was not only his air of smugness and obvious bad mood that was peeing her off but the fact he did not look much older than her as far as she could gauge. She began to wonder what he did for excitement if he wasn't keen on speed. His infernal references to Lewis Hamilton,

Ferraris, The Stig, and Top Gear were become more and more irritating. He constantly twiddled his pen through his fingers as he spoke. He tapped the table and the display screen with irritating frequency. His only redeeming feature was he bore a resemblance to Channing Tatum in Coach Carter, with his military style shaved head, and a physique to match. She tried to guess what colour his hair would be if he let it grow. His eyes were deep blue so she guessed he would be blond. He would probably look quite attractive if he could manage a smile, she thought.

Her mind began to drift from the points being made with the pen to other films that Channing had starred in. He'd definitely starred in *'Step Up'*. Was he married? Did he have a child, she pondered, unable to recollect any celebrity facts about him. She did recall that he'd starred in a modern version of Twelfth Night, *'She's the Man'*. She had converted many a surprised student with this film when they bemoaned how boring Shakespeare was.

Being put on the spot by Nick roused her from her daydreams. He was posing a question directly to her. "Erica! ERICA! Sorry to wake you love," he smiled condescendingly. Lowering his voice he continued. "We were trying to establish the maximum speed limit for a car towing a caravan on a dual carriageway," he prompted through gritted teeth.

"I don't have a caravan" she'd blurted, much to the amusement of the other candidates. She desperately tried to wrack her brains for an answer.

"One day you might though."

"Not likely!"

"Well play along for the purposes of this course please," he requested, firmly.

Erica sensed he was losing his patience. "Fifty miles per hour?" she offered tentatively. To her relief it was sufficient for Annoying Nick to raise his right hand to check his watch and allow them to have a break for coffee.

"Back here at 11.15" he ordered before marching out of the room.

As she sat on her own, drinking her tea, she doubted that Annoying Nick's bank balance would bear any resemblance to the famous actor's fortune rendering it insufficient for her to overlook his short comings. He was also far too serious and had obviously got out of bed the wrong side that morning.

By the time Annoying Nick checked his watch to announce the completion of the course, Erica begrudgingly had a greater awareness of her speed. The whole experience had come at a price: £100 course fee and four hours out of her schedule as a teacher to avoid paying a £100 fine and having three more points on her licence. The points had been creeping up to the danger zone and she couldn't afford to lose her licence. On reflection, missing double English and Twelfth Night with Year Ten to spend it with Annoying Nick was a price worth paying. Holding her tongue and eating humble pie had achieved the aim of no additional points on her licence.

Chapter 3

Saturday 5th August 2023

It had now been nearly four years since the experience, and she was *'pointless'* as her older brother, Tom, liked to remind her. Erica was having trouble reconciling how anyone would choose speed awareness as a career choice when the trusty sat nav advised once more of an approaching speed camera. She was still on cruise control and minding her own business in the slow lane as she was in no particular rush.

In no part to Annoying Nick, Erica had left in plenty of time from her home in Wiltshire. She was making good progress on her pilgrimage to the Writer's Summer School in the Derbyshire village of Swanwick. It was 10am on a warm, sunny Saturday in August, when she had turned out of Quantocks Drive in Melksham to begin the one-hundred-and-seventy-mile journey north to Derbyshire. She hoped to arrive by 3pm at the latest. The sat nav had informed her that, in current traffic conditions, it would take three hours and seventeen minutes to complete the journey. That allows for a couple of comfort breaks she thought as she joined the A350 towards Chippenham.

. . .

Creative writing had always been a hobby of Erica's and for the past year she had been working on a novel in the hope of becoming a published author. She was realistic in her expectations but dreamt that one day she might write a best seller. Her current novel was a personal story and she viewed it as a practice piece. Due to her work, her time was limited resulting in slow progress. She had subscribed to 'Writers Online' and saw their advertisement for The Writers' Summer School. In a bold moment, she had signed up.

Swanwick was advertised as, 'Possibly the oldest writing school of its type having been founded in 1948, and first held in 1949'. It appeared to have the potential to offer so much especially if the weather was warm and sunny. Thankfully the forecast was promising fine, warm weather and Erica began to relax into the drive. Daydreaming about walks around the lake, drinks on the lawn and the continuous round of workshops, talks and inspiration elicited a feeling of contentment mixed with apprehension. Erica was not a social butterfly.

Erica had spent the last two years saving as much of her teacher's salary as possible to provide a deposit for a home of her own whilst still making the most of her parents' hospitality. Finally, with a little extra assistance from them, she had enough deposit to be able to take on a two bedroomed shoe box on a new estate. The property was only three miles from her parents' house, but far enough away from her school to limit unnecessary contact with pupils and parents; an essential criterion when choosing her location.

. . .

At thirty years old Erica loved the newfound independence and freedom but yearned for someone with whom to share life's adventures. Most of Erica's friends were married or in relationships apart from Lucy who also desired to find Mr Right. Lucy shared the trials and tribulations of online dating, and they provided each other with moral support, honest feedback, and a shoulder to cry on when required.

Lucy was tall, naturally blond, bubbly, and confident whereas Erica was five foot four, bottle auburn, shy and socially insecure especially where men were involved. The opposite, however, was true once she walked on stage to perform and sing as a character in a show. Being someone else was always easier than being herself. Her hobby gave her the opportunity to perform and escape into a world where generally there were happy endings. Through her amateur dramatics she had built a circle of friends, but it hadn't yielded any suitable candidates for Mr Right, mainly due to the fact that the male thespians were either gay or married.

Lucy and Erica shared a sense of humour, caring nature, and a love of all things Disney. Lucy had a cat named Mufasa and Erica had *'Carla the Karma Llama'*. Carla was safely stowed in the boot on route to her next adventure that would be catalogued through photography in readiness for the start of term. Carla had previously visited Crete and Rhodes. Swanwick was going to be a stark contrast to the Greek Islands. The beloved class pet had surprisingly tolerated weekends away at various students' homes and her adventures were duly recorded in the class scrap book. Gone were the days of taking the class pet Gerbil home for the holidays and trying to keep it alive. Carla had been treated well for the most part but had needed some minor operations to close seams and restore her embroidered eyes. These had been skilfully performed by Erica's mother who was a dab hand with a needle and cotton, restoring Carla to full health. Her mother was unexpectedly invested in the project, encouraging Erica by rustling up a bikini, tropical garland, and sunglasses for Carla to wear whilst on her holidays. Erica did have concerns that the children had lost their grip on reality believing the Llama to be a living being.

Erica's phone pinged, announcing the arrival of a text message. No doubt it was Lucy providing an update on last night's date with Ryan the fitness freak, she guessed. This was her second date which was promising and a definite boost to morale. She looked forward to finding out more when she next stopped.

Erica was reminded of her own recent online dating experiences. She had tried a number of dating sites and was starting to despair. There had been no shortage of first dates. They were all very civilised affairs and mainly consisted of eating out or going for a walk. She had been through the awkward silences when she discovered that her date had nothing to talk about or any interest in her. One guy had called her by another girl's name, and another would not stop talking about himself. There had been the occasion when her date was unrecognisable compared to the profile picture on which she'd based her decision to meet up. She was almost relieved when the decision to not pursue a relationship was in her hands. There had, however, been a few dates when she felt that everything had gone well and was hopeful of a second date. She recalled the anticipation of waiting for a message requesting to meet again. She always left it a couple of days before making the first move, hoping that she would receive a reply. A pattern of ghosting had begun to emerge which knocked an already fragile self-belief. If she had been lucky, one or two had bothered to text to say that they weren't interested in pursuing anything, but the majority resorted to silence. This caused her to question why she wasn't interesting enough to the opposite sex. Despite her mother, brother, and Lucy's reassurances to the contrary, Erica was feeling dejected and rejected. She was looking forward to five days of escapism from the knock backs of dating apps. Why were single men always such selfish pricks? she asked herself.

Sat Nav brought her to reality with a request to get in lane to negotiate the transition onto the M42 which circumnavigated Birmingham. She really needed the loo and also wanted to check out the text from Lucy. A brief stop at Hopwood Park services provided the promised 'Welcome Break' and revealed that the text, as predicted, was from Lucy. Although Ryan the fitness fanatic couldn't understand why, Lucy was having doubts. Following text ping- pong, it was established that Ryan had a long history of flings, enjoyed talking about himself and gave off awkward vibes. Erica and Lucy concluded that Ryan was a narcissistic philanderer and potential cheat. They agreed that she wasn't that desperate, so Ryan was duly kicked into touch. Back to the drawing board for Lucy.

Duly relieved and updated Erica re-joined the M42. Her thoughts drifted to the novel that she yearned to finish and ultimately publish. She had been working on it for the previous year but had hit a brick wall, metaphorically speaking. She was hoping that she could be inspired to write the final chapters following this year's retreat. The heroine's back story was based on her own life whereas the Hero was undoubtedly an unrealistic creation and pure fantasy. The difficulty, she surmised, was that she had never met the 'one' to enable her to write him, whereas, she had plenty of material from her own experiences to write the heroine. Why was it that the only men in her life had been unmitigated disasters? It could all be so different if she was the heroine of her own novel. She let out a long audible sigh.

The benefit of the long drive up north was that she could mull things over without distractions. The drawback was that it evoked painful memories of what she had thought was her first real relationship.

Chapter 4

July 2014

Dean Scott was from Stoke on Trent and was staying at the same resort in Ibiza when they first met in July 2014. She was a 20-year-old university student attending her cousin's wedding, and he was a 22-year-old northern 'Cheeky Chappy' attending a stag do with his mates. His demeanour was charming in every way.

Ibiza was not her holiday destination of choice. She was there for the wedding and was trying to make the most of it. She was not into the club scene especially of the type on offer locally, but she was determined to enjoy herself. She was single but had her parents, aunt, and uncle and two cousins with her for company.

Erica had met Dee as he played pool with his friends in the Bar at their hotel. She had guessed he was around six feet tall as he looked similar to her brother, Tom. He had short brown hair and designer stubble. He probably just hadn't bothered shaving, she'd thought as she watched him flit around the pool table. He was wearing bright orange swim shorts and flip flops. His chest was bare and pale. He had a ring of suntan around his neck indicating that he rarely took off his top to expose himself to the rays of the sun. A red and white striped shield with 'The Potters' tattooed underneath branded him as a Stoke City FC supporter. He was not overweight but had the body of someone who shied away from exercise and ate too much fast food, she'd thought, as she observed his antics.

When he saw her, he had smiled cheekily before showing off his potting skills by clearing the table. As he re-racked the balls, he had asked her if she wanted to join in. She had declined, telling him that she was no good. He had practically pulled her off her feet as he dragged her to the table and gave her his cue. He had put his arm around her to help her with the cueing action making her blush with embarrassment as she was only wearing a bikini. This had continued as they played out the game which had resulted in another win for Dee. He flattered her and fetched her drinks from the 'all inclusive' bar. His mates were busy chatting to a hen party, so he'd suggested they should take a walk.

They had strolled, hand in hand on the long golden beach, pausing to sit and chat, finding out about each other. He had been single for a year after his girlfriend had cheated on him. He was 'between jobs' due to ill health but had recently worked in a casino. He had a flat in Hanley, Stoke on Trent, where he lived on his own and his parents and younger brother lived nearby. He implied that he was close to his family and valued family life. He had sounded like a normal young lad.

. . .

Holding hands and their first kiss couldn't have felt more romantic. She had believed that they had a connection. She spent the majority of her time in his shadow for the remainder of her holiday. He had made her feel special and she had high hopes that they would continue their relationship beyond Ibiza.

She'd been disappointed when he preferred to stay up all night and then wasted most of the day sleeping. She dreamt of exploring the area with him. In her naivety she had tolerated his lack of interest in cultural matters and attempted to fit in with his nocturnal habits. She couldn't keep up. She had got to the point where she would go to her own room around 2am and then spend the day sleeping on her sun lounger. At 7pm she would join him again for the evening. What he was doing all night had been a mystery to her.

She had no experience of the drug scene and was ignorant of the nightlife in Ibiza.

With hindsight, she had wasted a perfectly good holiday, and he was a waste of a perfectly good skin, she thought, noticing that her grip on the steering wheel had caused her knuckles to whiten.

They had, however, maintained contact until December of 2014.

The sat nav warned of yet another speed camera, as she continued to recall life with Dee.

Chapter 5

Saturday 19th December 2014

Hanley, Stoke on Trent

She spent her weekends driving up the motorway to the north to spend time with him. He was inexplicably reluctant to make any effort to travel and socialise with her and her housemates. Erica's visits had revolved around waiting for him to wake up, which was usually around 4pm and then sitting in the dingy gloom of his flat watching movies during the night. He always had to 'pop out' to help a mate, leaving her alone. Erica would nod off by midnight and he would still be up until 5am when he would finally pass out from whatever he had been consuming.

In the early days, Erica couldn't understand why he appeared to be drunk without having noticeably consumed any alcohol. He would appear chilled, and his eyes were bloodshot.

It finally became apparent that his nocturnal lifestyle was linked to his drug addiction and that he was a 'Medicine Man' to pay for his own Cannabis habit. There was a musky, herbal odour with an unpleasant undertone about him that she couldn't decipher. Eventually she dared to question him. First, he had mocked her innocence but then attempted to get her on side. "It's not 'hard' drugs just an occasional bit of Weed" he'd sneered. "Most people do it. It's not addictive" he had assured. "I helped out a mate and he paid me in Puff" he concluded matter-of-factly.

The fairy tale was morphing into a nightmare, and she desperately needed to wake up. Unfortunately, she had become trapped by his coercive and controlling nature. He was adept at playing her. Her natural caring disposition had left her vulnerable to his sob stories. He had the ability to tug at her heart strings and make her feel insensitive if she failed to comply. The rot set in when he claimed that he was on the verge of being evicted from his apartment. He blamed his situation on a delay in his housing benefit and other associated benefits being processed too slowly. "Of course I'll pay you back, as soon as the money comes through," he had pleaded. She had finally relented and transferred him the three thousand pounds he needed. Erica's great aunt had left her twelve thousand pounds in her will when she had died the previous year, so she dipped into that.

Unfortunately, the draining of her funds hadn't stopped there. Over the next couple of weeks, she handed over more and more. There was never any sign of the benefits being sorted and as a result no money found its way back into Erica's bank account. There was always a plausible reason why he needed more cash. It was only when she had threatened to leave him that he confessed to the 'real reason' for his desperation.

. . .

He had been entrusted with the delivery of a substantial package of drugs but en route he had been mugged by youths armed with knives. He was now being threatened by the hierarchy as he now owed them a considerable sum for losing their property and only had a short time to repay them what he owed.

This had been Erica's Epiphany. It was substantially too late to save her money, but she had no desire to become a gangster's moll. She had waited for him to become comatose. At 6am, ten thousand pounds down and her emotions in shreds she had grabbed her belongings and made her escape.

It had been a long, traumatic drive home. Thankfully it was daylight. Erica had no idea how she managed to see clearly to negotiate the never-ending journey back to the safety of her student accommodation. She had stormed through the front door and hurled herself onto her bed where all the supressed emotions exploded onto her pillow.

She stirred when her phone pinged to announce the arrival of a text. Why she had looked at it she did not know but there it was. 'Em *Where are you? Don't leave me – they're going to kill me – I am a dead man – I only need £600 – please help me ! D xx.'*

With hindsight, she should have replied *'good it'll save me a job!'*. She spent time thinking of all the alternative responses she could have made in an attempt to lighten her mood. But to no avail. Instead '*NO*' had been her succinct response.

. . .

He had upped the ante '*I can't go on without you! I love you! I'm sorry for everything! I'm going to kill myself.*' She had launched the handset across the room and stuck her head under the pillow attempting to hide from the situation.

When she had finally emerged, her eyes had been stinging and blood shot. Her face was a hot, damp, blotchy mess with her straggling red hair stuck to her cheeks. A military corps of drums beat a steady rhythm in her head, and she felt nauseous and alone. Her friends had already gone home for Christmas. No one was at home to share her pain.

She had finally bitten the bullet and called her brother.

Chapter 6

Sunday 20th December 2014

Keynsham, Bristol

It was 10.30am on, what was supposed to be, a lazy Sunday morning when Tom's phone jolted him awake. He had been taking advantage of a lie in with his long-term girlfriend, Laura. They were sleeping off a boozy night out with their university friends, some of whom were asleep on the floor in the lounge. He juggled the phone to his ear to be greeted by incoherent sobs and garbled words. If it hadn't been for the fact that Erica's name had appeared on his phone, he would have struggled to know who he was listening to. It was apparent to Tom that something awful had happened and now was not the moment for jesting. He was becoming more alert and quickly processing how to approach his sister's hysteria. "Hey Sis! Slow down! Just answer Yes or No – Are you injured?"

"No."

"Have you crashed the car?"

"No."

"Are you at your digs?"

"Yes." Relief washed over him as he tried to soothe Erica to the point where she could coherently explain her situation.

With the obvious causes eliminated he puzzled as to what could be the problem.

"Is it Dee related?" he ventured.

"Yes" she spluttered.

"Oh Ok, now we're getting somewhere," Tom soothed. Relationship guidance was not his strong point. Tom was fortunate to have been in a stable relationship with Laura since school and throughout university. They were soul mates as well as lovers and appeared destined to be together forever. He hadn't had the experience of a turbulent love life so didn't feel qualified to impart words of wisdom to his, obviously traumatised, sister. A first time for everything, he thought. Digging deep, he ventured "Have you split up?"

"Yes" her reply was soft and sad. The closed questions appeared to be having the desired effect of quelling her emotions.

"Did he hit you?"

"No." she wailed.

Trying to inflect lightness into his voice he responded, "Ah! Good! Good! That's a relief! Are you able to tell me more?"

Amongst intermittent sobs and whimpers, Erica poured out the whole story. Tom attempted to comprehend the enormity of his sister's naivety and vulnerability. All the while, he wrestled with the urge to shout, *You bloody idiot! Just do the maths! How many years would it take for him to repay that sort of 'loan'! Surely you realised he was all about the drugs? Couldn't you see the signs? Why? Why? Why?* But on this occasion, he knew well enough to hold back and let her continue uninterrupted.

Laura silently slipped him a mug of tea and mouthed, *tell me later*, before heading down to their guests who were stirring in the lounge. Tom adjusted the pillows and sat upright to drink the tea while listening to the story unfold. He sipped it as quietly as he could knowing that the slightest slurp usually triggered an angry reaction from Erica who was hypersensitive to noisy eaters and drinkers. Then again, she had *'bigger fish to fry'* and hopefully wouldn't even notice. He subconsciously fiddled with the chain around his neck as he listened.

"So now it's confirmed that I'm a certifiable idiot," she concluded, providing the cue for a response from her unusually subdued brother.

"I honestly don't know what to say!" was his immediate lame response. "What an absolute 'bar steward', scumbag, lowlife, vermin..." he paused not really knowing what else would do justice to the description of the bloke. "Sis, it's not your fault and I'm so, so, angry that someone has taken advantage of you. I know it's easy for me to say but you're better off without him. He's a classic druggy who will threaten to kill himself to keep you on his side. Hard as it is you've got to ignore him and block his number. DON'T send him anymore money," he instructed trying to sound in control of the situation.

"I haven't got any more to give him," she wailed as the reality sank in. "I've been such a fool and don't know what to do? Are you at home?"

"Yes, we're here." He paused, "Get yourself over here if you can concentrate enough to drive safely and we'll talk more about it if you want to!"

Tom was twenty-two and had finished his accountancy degree at Bristol University earlier in the year and was taking his time finding employment. He was living in a shared house with Laura, Matt, and Ed, on the outskirts of the city of Bristol, in Keynsham. Erica was twenty and in her second year at Bath Spa University. She was sharing a house with two lads and two girls in 'bedsit land' or Oldfield Park as it was officially called, in a suburb of Bath. It was approximately a twenty-minute drive to Tom's.

"Thanks, I'll have a shower and head over so probably see you at lunchtime – Oh! And please don't tell Mum and Dad" she begged.

"No problem – go carefully – see you shortly" he concluded, and they ended the call.

Tom threw on his joggers and a T shirt that were strategically placed on his *'floordrobe'*, adjusted his St Christopher which had become twisted, and joined the others in the lounge. He was struggling to shake off living the student life. Matt, Ed, and Laura were each on their second mug of tea and were eagerly awaiting an update. The others had decided that it was better that they headed on their way. Tom obliged and gave a summary of what had occurred to his attentive audience who, for once, sat in stunned silence until he finished. A cacophony of expletives filled the room and varied descriptions and insults were hurled at the absent villain.

"Hey guys, I've got a baseball bat," Ed announced to the room whilst tapping an imaginary bat in the palm of his hand as menacingly as he could. "Have you got this guy's address Tom?"

"I've got fuel in my car, let's get going and sort the f****r out," added Matt jumping to his feet with his car keys at the ready.

"Hey guys! Much as I appreciate your solidarity for Sis, I think this needs thinking through! First of all, I would get great satisfaction from kneecapping the lowlife scumbag, but I don't particularly want to do time for the little s**t! Second, Erica's on her way over and I don't think she'd be too chuffed if I wasn't here! Third, we're no professional vigilantes and would probably cock it up big time and be on some gangs hit list for the rest of our lives, and have to change our appearance, and get new identities!" He caught his breath before adding "I think it best if we just wait until the dust has settled."

Ed and Matt dropped back on to their seats and Laura nodded in agreement with Tom. "Bacon butties anyone? An army marches on its stomach," she joked in an attempt to raise their spirits and marched towards the kitchen.

Ed and Matt continued to discuss how they might teach the *scum bag* a lesson. They had learnt to fight back from a young age as they'd both been bullied at school and, occasionally at university. Tom had been known to stand up to anyone who stepped out of line, but he was the more passive of the three. Between them they were no pushover, but they weren't thugs. Most of their aggression was channelled on the rugby field most weekends.

Erica had not been in the mood for eating when she had arrived at midday but gratefully grasped the large mug of tea that was thrust into her hands by Laura. Ed and Matt had sensitively gone out for the afternoon to give the siblings space to discuss what needed to be discussed and after a short spell of sympathetic words and gestures, Laura had given Erica a hug and headed into the city to do some window shopping.

Tom had waited until everyone had left before attempting to unpick the situation. Erica had looked exhausted and on the verge of tears without anything being said, so Tom abandoned the chat and gave her a rare hug, which set her off again. It had proved to be more tea and sympathy than a resolution to the situation. "Thank you for being here for me," she convulsed.

"That's what big brothers are for Sis," he'd quipped whilst fighting back his own rising emotions. She managed a watery hint of a smile and quietly sipped the last of her, now cold, tea.

There were numerous things that Tom had wanted to say to Erica but none of them would have been helpful in that moment. Useless phrases kept jumping into his head, *No point crying over spilt milk, plenty more fish in the sea. One day we'll look back on this and laugh,* but instead he kept his arm around her and said "Look! The guy is a junky- fact! You weren't to know that! – fact, he manipulated you because you have a good heart and caring soul – fact, you have nothing to be ashamed of. Much as I'd like to go after the lowlife, there's nothing any of us can do to retrieve the money so we'll have to come up with a plan to rebuild your savings somehow, over time." He was on a roll and hoping that what he was saying was sensitive enough. "Don't let him 'win' by letting it drag you down! Don't waste your energy on what's happened. Focus on what your future is going to be! You'll eventually meet a decent bloke, have a successful career, and achieve whatever you put your mind to!"

As Erica had melted into more tears, Tom realised that it would most likely take a while for his words and advice to be fully appreciated, but he had tried his best.

Tom was quietly relieved to be interrupted by the return of Laura who heaved her rucksack through the door and plonked it on the floor. "Thought this might come in handy?" she announced as she ceremoniously placed two bottles of Malbec and a case of Peroni in the centre of the coffee table, along with various crisps and snacks. "I thought you might prefer to stop over, Erica?" Attempting to brighten up, Erica had smiled pathetically and agreed.

"I don't have any lectures, it's the Christmas holidays, so if you really don't mind that would be nice. Sorry to be such a pain." She had spoken quietly and was obviously fighting hard not to dissolve into yet more floods of tears.

Tom sent a text to Ed and Matt giving them the 'all clear' to return should they wish and gave them the heads up that Erica would be kipping on the sofa that evening. Tom had known Matt and Ed throughout his four years at university and they were the best of friends. "Such a shame it turned out Matt and Ed are gay," he whispered to Laura as they stood in the kitchen on the pretext of putting the shopping away. "One of them would have been a perfect distraction for Erica! I just wish she would get out more to meet genuine people. You'd have thought there would be one half decent bloke on her course or somewhere on the campus." They shared a look of disappointment before re-entering the scene of mourning in the lounge to try and arrange a takeout for dinner. Erica had nodded off and was purring softly on the sofa. Considering himself to be an expert, through his intimate knowledge of his sister's takeout preferences formulated over the last twenty years, Tom took the gamble and ordered Dominoes pizzas to be delivered at 7.30pm.

It was now 6pm and Tom took the opportunity to shower and mulled over the events of the previous few hours. Annoying as she can be, he'd thought, she doesn't deserve this. He'd been taken aback at the eagerness with which his best friends had risen to Erica's defence and shocked by the lengths to which they appeared to want to go to settle the situation. His own sensible brain was now fighting hard against his reactive brain that was plotting revenge as he vigorously lathered up and rinsed. Deep in thought, he'd been interrupted by Laura who, in a stage whisper, implored him to hurry up as the steam was permeating the rest of the upstairs and at risk of setting off the very sensitive smoke detector.

As he stepped onto the shower mat and reached for his towel, he knew that the matter required intricate planning.

Chapter 7

5th August 2023

On reflection, Erica couldn't believe how gullible she'd been. She breathed deeply trying to stem the flood of emotion which was forcing its way from her stomach to her eyes. "Get a grip," she yelled in an attempt to dissipate the unwanted feelings. Her brain was relentless, and she couldn't stop the memories from swamping her whole being as she continued her journey.

Had it really been nine years since all this happened, she questioned herself. She felt embarrassment and anger as she recalled the sordid details of this episode of her life. Tom had been her rock then and since which was surprising to her as their early teenage years had been spent fighting and tormenting each other. He was a windup merchant, and she was highly strung. He lit the fuse, and she exploded on cue. The more she exploded the more fuses he lit. Erica couldn't remember the moment that they had declared a cease fire and become allies, but she was relieved that they had. He could still be extremely annoying under the guise of *'friendly banter'* which wasn't always appreciated. She had taught herself not to rise to the bait but occasionally she got caught, much to Tom's immense pleasure and her disgust! Overall though they had each other's backs, and on that occasion, she had needed him big time.

Erica had used the majority of her experience as the plot for her novel. Unleashing the episode had proved to be traumatic yet cathartic and she was creeping closer to forgiving herself for being such an imbecile. Erica did, however, worry that Dee would recognise himself in her book. She had taken the usual precautions of changing his name and hers. She had tried using anagrams in an attempt to be clever but there were too few letters to work with. She wasn't sure if naming him Richard was too flippant, but she savoured the idea of shortening it to *'Dick'*. On second thoughts, what were the chances of him recognising anything? Would he have enough braincells left to read? Would he still be alive? She therefore dismissed any concerns that the low life, scum bag, as Tom had called him, would be any the wiser. She would add the disclaimer that 'any resemblance to persons living, or dead was purely coincidental,' which seemed to be standard for any work of fiction.

She was still deciding what name she wanted her heroine to have and had been enjoying searching for one that she liked. Stacey was her current favourite. More than one person had told her she bore a resemblance to Stacey Dooley, so it was as good a reason as any.

Stacey was going to achieve what she hadn't been able to and that was sweet revenge. It was going to conclude with her finding Mr Right and living happily ever after.

. . .

It had given Erica a sadistic pleasure trying to work out the details of her revenge. She had spent a long time running through many alternative scenarios, some of which had shocked her in their gangland brutality! She had tried to rope in Tom to give her some ideas, but he had been reluctant to contribute. He did, however, recount the reactions of Matt and Ed on that December evening in 2014 and suggested it could form the basis of a possible revenge attack. It dawned on Erica that her search history could be seriously misinterpreted should she ever be investigated. A sinister smile crept across her face as she revelled in the pleasure it was giving her. Good job no one can see me, she thought as she checked her mirrors before signalling to change lanes. I must look like a psychopath.

She was conscious of the fact that whatever course of action Stacey took, it had to be realistic and forensically sound. She had therefore, booked a one-to-one session with a lecturer whose specialism was *'Crime Writing – How to Get away with Murder'*. According to his profile, Richard Noyles was new to the Writing School but had done the rounds on the writing circuit. His website portrait showed a guy with blue eyes, an unruly mop of fair hair and a medium stubble beard. He was thirty-six years old and looked a fairly fit specimen from Erica's viewpoint. She was strangely excited but apprehensive at the prospect of meeting Mr Noyles. She was anticipating he would be able to help her plot Stacey's revenge. I really mustn't forget that I'm writing fiction though, she instructed herself.

. . .

A long blast from an Eddie Stobart truck jolted her to reality, preventing her from straying into the centre lane and causing an incident. She hadn't realised how absorbed she had been in her macabre plans or how supressed her feelings had been throughout the last nine years.

Sat Nav advised her to prepare to join the M1 signalling that her journey was nearing its conclusion. It was just as well that she had been distracted from her ponderings as she would, without doubt, have ended up heading south to Leicester rather than north to Alfreton. She was now in new territory. Her previous jaunts beyond Birmingham had only taken her to the drug troubled, Monkey Dust capital of the UK, the City of Stoke Upon Trent. She sincerely hoped that The Writer's Summer School, would prove to be the antithesis.

Check-in to the Hayes conference centre was seamless and Erica steadily dragged her luggage to her ground floor room. She had been placed in the modern Lakeside block on the opposite side of the campus to the old, main house. Shoving her door with her shoulder, she propped it open with her case while she put the key card in the slot to activate the electricity. Not bad, she thought as she made her way across the room to the window to get her bearings. She had a view of the car park and some cows in a field. She prioritised by filling the kettle before unpacking her belongings and Carla. The crisp white sheets, teal cushions and throw brought to mind a Premier Inn. One advantage of being single, she mused, I don't have to share the bed! Having tested the bed with a jig up and down, her eyes delighted upon the individually wrapped biscuits which reminded her that she had not eaten since breakfast. She tore one open and munched hungrily whilst setting up her laptop. She posed Carla for a working photo at the keyboard followed by one of her enjoying a biscuit with a cup of tea.

Erica collapsed into the armchair with her phone to text her mother and Tom. *'Sat nav and St Christopher have performed well and brought me safely to Derbyshire, having a cup of tea, got to meet up at 4.30, will keep you posted... love you xx'*. Both she and Tom had received Saint Christopher necklaces for their eighteenth birthdays and had felt compelled to wear them whenever a journey was being undertaken. This was more to please their mother than personal belief in the powers of the patron saint of travellers. Erica gently kissed the pendant and whispered, "Thank you," as she always did on arrival at her destination. "You've not let me down yet."

Sipping her tea and reading through the literature she had been handed on arrival, Erica noted that Richard Noyles was scheduled to deliver his specialist course the following morning. Taking one of her new highlighter pens, bought especially for this occasion, she drew a yellow line across the entry to ensure that she did not overlook it. She would have fun later on using the different coloured pens to colour code all the sessions that she wanted to attend. She was already beginning to enjoy herself and the feeling of being the new kid joining school, was exciting. She would also have to organise her new *school bag* with her stationery and notebooks prior to the sessions tomorrow. Tucking her 'Guide to Summer School' into an easily accessible pocket, Erica queried when her obsession for all things stationery had first started. She recalled her primary school teacher reporting to her parents that she was obsessed with erasers when she was six years old. Could that have been the start? She chuckled to herself as she pictured herself deliberately making errors with her pencil in order to have to rub them out, much to the dismay of Mr Collins. Quite a harmless obsession compared to some of the kids at my school, she thought.

As a newbie, she had been given two lanyards for her name badge. To distinguish her from other regular '*Swanickers*' one was teal and the other white. She would be recognised as a novice should she choose to wear the white one and presumably receive assistance and understanding from the old timers present, if required. She opted to wear them both to begin with. A reception for newbies was scheduled for 4.30pm where there would be an introductory talk and welcome by the Chair of Summer School. Erica glanced at her watch which informed her that she had an hour to kill before the reception. She opted to shower and change. A notice on the door advised her to keep the bathroom door shut while using the shower. This was to prevent the fire detector from being activated. Taking extra care, she double checked the door before taking her shower. She finally emerged from her room refreshed and ready to face the other delegates with the sprinkler system intact.

She turned right out of her room and ambled along the corridor to the foyer where there was a settee and a coffee table. The door to the right led out to the carpark and the door on the left opened out onto the main campus. Erica wandered through the door to the main campus and strolled along the path which led passed the accommodation block. She stopped to take in the scene.

. . .

To her left, a path descended gently towards the lake. On its route was another entrance to the Lakeside and beyond that were some conference facilities. In front of her and to the left of the path were the formal gardens which swept up to the main house. The main house was far bigger than she had expected. It was typically Victorian in appearance with dark aging brick-work. Multiple chimney stacks stood either side of a central light-coloured belfry. She could make out the arched windows of the Vinery with its pitched roof to the left of a more modern, glass fronted annex, which she guessed was the Garden Lounge. Renovations were underway judging by the scaffolding that was scarring the scene. She could see bay windows on two levels and smaller attic windows nestled in the roof. As she continued slowly, she noted that the church was up the path to her right. She was curious to look inside but time was against her. A short distance later, she passed the Main Lecture Hall which stood on its own, a few steps from the entrance to the covered concourse that led to the main house. Inside the concourse she noted more conference rooms, toilets and two dining areas. She finally arrived in front of the Bar and found herself in the Garden Lounge overlooking the lawns. The light beige carpet gave way to a terracotta, herringbone tiled floor in the Vinery which was furnished appropriately with white wicker chairs, tables, and a variety of house plants.

Erica noted other people wandering around with their maps in hand and wearing the white lanyards. She turned back into the area housing the bar. Plenty of coffee machines were strategically placed next to the bar and in the area to the right, that ultimately led to the reception area. Beyond the bar area the new blended into old via the Vinery or the reception area, depending on which route you chose.

The welcome venue was nearby in a grand lounge reminiscent of an old country house or old fashioned, *'gentlemen's club'*. Erica had entered via the Vinery through one of many archways, passing a sweeping staircase before entering the lounge between two marble pillars that appeared to be supporting the ceiling. There were a couple of trestle tables covered with white tablecloths upon which were wine glasses waiting to welcome the newbies. A mixture of wingback fireside chairs and Chesterfield type settees were filling up with delegates. A wing back chair was empty, so she dropped her bag on the floor and sat down, grateful that she would not have to sit next to a stranger. From her position she surveyed her surroundings further. The high white ceilings were divided by a lattice of oak beams. In the centre of each square was a shape which housed a light. There were circles, crosses, stars, and shapes she did not even know. The lower walls were panelled with oak and there were fancy carvings above the imposing wide doors that led off the room. She lowered her gaze and was mesmerised by the pale yellow and brown waves on the greyish blue carpet.

Huddles had formed of people she assumed must know each other already. The sound of chatter and laughter reverberated. "Hi, I'm Glenda Allot," announced a tall, blond, slender official whose badge communicated that she was an 'ambassador and author'. Erica attempted to stand to shake hands.

"Erica, Erica Mills," she responded as Glenda signalled for her to remain seated. Erica observed that she looked smart in her navy-blue trousers, fitted jacket and a Joules striped top. They exchanged pleasantries and Glenda explained her role. As an experienced Swanicker she was tasked with providing guidance to newbies if required and was also leading one of the specialist courses. Glenda ensured that a glass of red wine headed Erica's way before moving on to the next white lanyard.

Erica was not good at social situations which required her to make the first move, so she stayed in her chair to quietly observe the proceedings from a safe distance. Apprehension was setting in and she began to wonder how she was going to cope with the next four days. She clung to her glass with one hand and the guide in the other in a vain attempt to look occupied.

"Watchya," boomed a larger-than-life character who peered closely to read her name badge, "Erica."

"Hi!" she croaked feebly, feeling trapped in her restricted personal space. Sensing her discomfort, the owner of the booming voice turned down the volume and continued to introduce himself as Barry G Sheldon, Chair of the Summer School Committee. He placed great emphasis on the *G* so as not to confuse him with all the other Barry Sheldons, she thought to herself. He too was an ambassador and a published author. He proceeded to explain the history of the school to Erica. She listened, politely nodding at suitable intervals to convince him of her interest. She wondered if she had visibly winced when he had first boomed at her as he was now a few decibels quieter.

According to Tom, her brother, she was not very good at disguising her feelings. Tom would be in his element pressing the flesh and networking, she thought woefully. How can we be so different? Barry thankfully moved on to deafen another victim. She couldn't help being reminded of the actor, Brian

Blessed. She warned herself to be careful not to accidentally call him Brian when they next met.

Relief flowed over Erica when it was finally announced that the Vice Chair of School was about to make a welcome speech to all the assembled delegates. At least now I won't have to talk to anybody else for a bit, she thought gratefully. As Evelyn Napier began her prepared speech, welcoming everyone to the 74th annual Writers' Summer School at The Hayes, Swanwick, Erica planned her next move.

The sun was still shining, and daylight hours were plenty. A walk around the lake with Carla was currently the most appealing option for after dinner. She would then attend the evening session at 8pm which was being led by the poet, Ria Ambrose-Picton. She thought of dinner with mixed emotions. She was famished but was now hearing that there would be a specific table for all new delegates set aside for the first dinner of the week.

It was 5.30pm as the vice chair wound up her speech by wishing everyone an enjoyable and creative few days. Erica thrust her paperwork into her bag and swung it onto her shoulders to free up her hands. Picking up her glass she rushed to return it to the bar before heading back to her room. The bar area was filling up as more delegates were arriving and catching up with old friends. Erica made a beeline for the counter and deposited her glass. As she spun around to leave, she accidentally clobbered someone with her rucksack. Uttering an apology, she realised with horror that her victim was Richard Noyles.

"Oh! I'm so sorry" she gushed. "Have I hurt you?" she checked, making brief eye contact. He looked at her, his eyes wide with shock.

"No love," he assured her "I'm ok Erica."

"That's good then." She hesitated, glancing at him before concluding "Must dash, sorry again!"

She could feel his eyes boring into her as she strode off in the direction of her room. Not the best start to the week, she thought as she let herself into the Lakeside.

This week is going to be challenging in more ways than one, she thought as she marched to the safety of her room.

Sitting in the sanctuary of her room, Erica took the opportunity to update Lucy on her day via text message. She recounted the embarrassing first encounter with Richard and Lucy responded with three laughter emojis and a X. Using their WhatsApp family group, she sent everyone a video of her surroundings and a photo of Carla lying on the bed. Reassuringly, everyone responded promptly with a heart emoji and a couple of Xs. As usual, her mother replied with a short message *'Hope you and Carla have a great time and come home a best-selling author! X'*. Feeling supported from afar, Erica checked her appearance in the mirror. She hoped that her denim jeggings and loose long shirt were suitable for evening wear. Stuffing Carla into her rucksack she set off to experience her first Swanwick dinner.

The smell that was wafting along the corridor reminded her of school dinners, as did the queue that was already forming. She dutifully took her place and waited patiently. She could hear the growing buzz of delegates catching up having, presumably, not seen each other for twelve months. The line progressed to the long-awaited buffet counter where she chose lasagne and received her ration of one slice of garlic bread. Clutching her plate, she gingerly looked around for the aforementioned newbies table. She was relieved to see that there were no spaces left. Instead, she opted for a seat at the end of a table set for eight that was currently unoccupied. If I eat quickly enough, she thought, I can be finished before anyone joins me.

Glancing around furtively, she noticed a table that was occupied by *'Brian Blessed'*, *'slender Glenda'*, Evelyn and others who she assumed to be Swanwick hierarchy. There was no sign of Richard Noyles. She devoured her dinner and savoured the one piece of garlic bread whilst trying not to look as though she was stuffing her face. She was still hungry. It's going to be a while until breakfast, she justified to herself, as she went in search of pudding. Returning to her seat that was reserved by her rucksack, she was mortified to see that Richard Noyles had parked himself in the seat opposite hers. Her eyes swiftly scanned him. He was simply dressed, in dark blue straight legged shorts and a relaxed fit, white polo shirt. The whiteness of his shirt showed off his muscular tanned arms which bore a smart watch on his right wrist and a leather plaited bracelet on the left. He looked the epitome of catalogue smart casual with his brown leather sandals finishing the look. She was now in a dilemma and scrolled through her options. She could sit opposite him and potentially dribble custard down her front; or worse, spill it over his pristinely white top; or she could find another empty table to guzzle her crumble and custard. She could then retrieve her bag on the pretext that she had left it behind. Before she could decide Richard spotted her and beckoned her over. As she got nearer, he smiled and pointed to her seat.

"Is that your weapon of mass destruction?"

She realised that he was referring to her rucksack and the

earlier incident.

"Yes" she responded nervously. "I was just getting pudding; I hadn't forgotten it". She felt like a child making excuses to her teacher. Taking great care not to spill anything, she reluctantly sat down to finish her meal. She was at a loss what to talk about so remained silent as she delicately consumed her pudding. She was conscious of the fact that he was looking at her as he chewed on his piece of garlic bread, but she did not want to make eye contact. Drawing breath as though he was about to say something, her phone rang with impeccable timing. "Do excuse me," she said as she dropped her spoon into the bowl and grappled with her bag to retrieve her handset. She looked at the screen while hastily standing up and swung her bag onto her shoulder, taking care not to attack anyone else with it. "I really have to take this, sorry."

Silencing the ring tone, she put the phone to her ear, "Hi! Thanks for getting back to me, just give me a moment as I'm in a noisy room." She wove her way through the tables and exited to the safety of the grounds. Once seated on a convenient bench, she put her phone back in her bag. She had never been more grateful to receive a junk phone call.

What's the matter with me, she thought, breathing deeply a few times to calm herself. Why am I so nervous? She was struggling to determine if it was being on her own at Swanwick that was affecting her or just Richard Noyles. She was definitely well out of her comfort zone and was starting to doubt if she would last the distance.

. . .

She had travelled alone and lived amongst strangers for far longer than this she reminded herself. She had survived for three months backpacking across Australia and New Zealand as well as touring the USA and Canada. She had been home sick and missed her family but had managed to make friends eventually with people in her group whilst away. What was causing her such anxiety? she pondered.

Being awkward amongst strangers was nothing new to Erica. She surmised that she was feeling intimidated by her perceived inferiority amongst so many accomplished literary types. Why am I always worried about making a fool of myself, she questioned. She could not help feeling that she had not made a good impression since arriving.

More people were starting to exit the dining hall and were making their way into the gardens to enjoy the evening sunshine before the final session of the day. It was going to take her time to settle into the hustle and bustle of Swanwick life, she thought to herself.

Erica picked up her bag and set off to follow the signs to the lake where she hoped to have some quiet time to herself with Carla. The sunlight was dancing off the lake and patches of cerise and white water lilies adorned the surface. She scanned the perimeter for people before making her way to the far side where she found a vacant bench. Feeling more relaxed, Erica retrieved Carla and strategically place her for her photo shoot by the lake. The lilies provided a perfect background for an arty shot of Carla. She took a couple of selfies with the Karma Llama and on her own before settling back down to enjoy the peace and tranquillity. She was reminded of fairy tales. Closing her eyes, she tilted her head upwards to feel the fading warmth of the evening sun. Thoughts whirled around as she soaked up the moment. Princes and Frogs - Why do my frogs never turn into princes? I haven't even kissed enough frogs to improve my chances- how did Richard know my name? She came too with a jump before she started down a 'rabbit hole' in an Alice in Wonderland moment. Her subconscious had taken her back to the incident in the bar, and she was sure that he had called her by name.

Glancing at her watch, Erica realised that it was time she made her way to the main hall for the evening's guest speaker. She didn't have time to get back to her room, so she made her way directly to the hall via the 'ladies'. Ensuring she got a seat at the back, Erica slid to the end so that she would not have to get up and down to let others in. At 8pm on the dot, Barry (*better not forget the G*) Sheldon stood at the front ready to announce the guest speaker. Erica was relieved that he chose to rely on his *Brian Blessed* voice rather than amplify it with the sound system that had been set up for his use.

"It gives me great pleasure to introduce to you our first guest speaker of the week who is a well-respected poet and performer. We're looking forward to hearing about you, Ria, and your poetic journey. Thank you for sparing some time to share your experience with us this evening. Please give a big Swanwick welcome to Ria Ambrose-Picton." His voice reached a crescendo, reminiscent of a boxing match compere.

. . .

Polite applause rippled as Ria settled in front of the microphone to commence her presentation. Erica had never heard of her but judging by the number of people in the hall, she was extremely popular. Ria looked typically Bohemian with long, wavy, henna dyed hair. She wore a floaty Indian print maxi dress that was accessorised with a long string of wooden beads. Large, brightly coloured, teardrop earrings swung as she moved her head while speaking. All she needed to complete the look was a daisy chain crown, thought Erica, who adored the look.

"Thank you, Barry and Swanwickers, for your warm welcome," she began with a broad smile. "I like to believe that there is a poet hidden away in all of us just waiting to be awakened," she suggested, in a voice reminiscent of the comedienne, Sarah Millican which made Erica anticipate that she would automatically be humorous.

Poetry was something that Erica turned to in her melancholy moments. She was, what she termed a traditional poet, writing poems that rhymed. She never shared these poems with others as they would open the window to her soul. In brighter times, her talent had been exploited on a number of occasions by her school. She had been commissioned to write poems for the students to perform for the school show and, more recently, Armistice Day. That was the only time she went public and usually to high acclaim.

Her view of performance styles had, much to her surprise, recently been broadened listening to Dr John Cooper Clarke perform. He had been the '*dictionary corner*' guest on 'Eight out of Ten Cats Does Countdown,' but she still preferred the more traditional style.

Now as she listened to Ria, she found unexpected pleasure learning about *'List'* poems. She had heard about the concept as a teacher of English but had never bothered to pursue it. Her perception had been that, if you recited your shopping list in a dramatic style it could be classed as a poem. In her mind she likened it to Picasso and impressionism of which she was not a fan.

Her eyes were being opened to the concept and she actually started to find the idea fun. Ria gave some examples of children's list poems and how to write them. Scribbling madly in her new notebook, Erica attempted to capture the essence of the style. 'Create an opening, find some rhyming words that can be used at the end of a line whilst adding others before them; close with a funny ending.' It all made sense to her in that moment, and she hoped that it would remain so until she had a chance to practice. It's been worth attending just for that she thought while imagining her year eight class's choice of rhyming words.

Ria's final section explored the use of her name to inspire creativity. She explained that her first name was of Spanish origin and translated as *'small river'*. It could be used to evoke characteristics of tranquillity, flowing streams, and carving out a path in life. Having *'an innate calm and sense of place'* she had been *'inspired in life to go with the flow whilst navigating obstacles that arose along the way'*. Erica was impressed with the analogy and the convenience of such a name. Unsurprisingly, as with many poets, Ria had faced numerous challenges that she now shared with her audience. Many of these struggles had been encapsulated by poetry and published in collections which were on sale in the Swanwick bookshop.

Erica wondered what her own name meant. She made a note to look it up later and to take a look in the bookshop.

As the floor was opened up for questions, Erica decided that she would make her exit. Quietly standing up she slipped through a gap in the chairs and crept to the door. It was getting dark but was still warm. She was starting to feel the effects of a very long day and turned left to make her way to the Lakeside accommodation.

She had barely taken two steps when she was intercepted by a woman with long raven hair who floated towards her in a ditsy patterned, mustard coloured, gypsy style dress and leather flip flops. She sported a white lanyard which was tangled in her beaded necklace and carried a large, knitted cotton tote bag. "Don't suppose you fancy joining me for a nightcap in the bar, do you?" she asked with a smile, indicating with her thumb the proposed direction of travel. "I could really do with a drink, and I don't know anyone - do you?" Before waiting for an answer, she hooked up Erica's arm stating, "If we get a move on, we should beat the rush!"

Seemingly having little choice in the matter, Erica complied with the request and found herself sitting on a two-seater sofa sipping a large glass of malbec courtesy of Dora. Dora led the conversation and Erica soon found herself relaxing as they discussed their favourite TV shows. She learned that Dora was a huge fan of anything to do with fictional and real-life crime. They both enjoyed watching 'Caught on CCTV' and 'Britain's most Evil Killers' amongst others. They agreed that presenter Fred Dineage must be getting on a bit and always had a tan. They were both in awe of his varied career and that he had met and written about the Kray twins.

Whilst Erica did not usually read crime stories, she was informed that Dora's love of crime fiction had started with John Grisham, Agatha Christie, Anthony Horowitz, and Ann Cleeves. More recently Dora had discovered Evelyn Napier and was excited to meet her in person at the Summer School. Evelyn was an accomplished author who set her crime thrillers in the city of Cardiff. Dora was familiar with the city which added to her enjoyment of the plots.

Erica explained that she had not intended including crime in her plot but was hoping to have some inspiration for *'bumping off'* or *'getting revenge'* on her antihero. She gave Dora a brief outline of the plot so far, explaining how it was based on personal experience. Dora's eyes lit up with excitement. She was a *'Wannabe'* writer of crime fiction and offered to help if she could. "I'd love to help you dispose of that miscreant," she said, rubbing her hands together. "It sounds like you could do with finding a decent bloke, but it must be difficult to trust anyone when you've been through that nightmare." She smiled sympathetically at Erica.

. . .

The bar had filled up quickly and the atmosphere was lively with excited chatter. Erica was beginning to feel less nervous and relieved that she had found an ally. She quickly surveyed the room and could not see Richard Noyles. Why she was even bothered about his whereabouts, she did not know.

The malbec was hitting the spot and she listened to Dora explain the trials and tribulations of her messy divorce from her controlling husband Craig, two years ago. Dora had come out of the mess with the family home in Clifton, Bristol, her seventeen-year-old daughter Grace, and a Dachshund named Frankfurter, or Frank for short. Apparently, Grace did not live up to her name and Frank was adorable.

"One for the road?" Dora asked springing to her feet with her empty glass in hand.

Erica glanced at the clock on the wall which informed her that it was 10.15pm and that her bed would be beckoning. She paused briefly holding her glass to defend it from attack. Dora was reaching forward to retrieve the glass and it seemed futile to put up a fight. Instead, she began to rise and heard herself responding, "Go on then if you insist. But it's my round please." Holding her hands out to relieve Dora of her glass she asked, "Same again?"

Dora smiled, nodded "Why not," and sat down leaving Erica to find her way through the crowded room to the bar. There was still no sign of Richard, so Erica felt safe from any potential embarrassment as she ordered and returned with two more malbecs. I don't want to be chucking these over anyone tonight, she thought recalling his and her white tops as she manoeuvred through the throng.

. . .

Dora was in full swing regaling another delegate about Craig, Grace, and Frank. Erica carefully placed the glass in front of her before taking her place on the sofa. She slowly sipped as she waited for Dora to resume their conversation. Fiddling with her lanyard and glancing at the badge attached to it, she had a sudden realisation. Earlier, Richard must have read her badge and that was how he knew her name. Why am I still thinking about him she queried, as Dora returned her attention to Erica.

"Thanks for the drink," Dora gushed as she took an enthusiastic glug. "Such interesting people." She referred to the couple who had escaped and headed off to their room. "They come here together as their annual holiday you know," she informed caressing her glass gently. Adopting a stage whisper, she leaned into Erica, "Not exactly an alternative to an All Inclusive in the Med!" She smirked as she put down her glass.

Not sure how to react, Erica quietly responded "Each to their own."

Last orders were called at 11pm. Erica was relieved when Dora agreed that it was probably time that they finished their drinks and headed to bed. Breakfast was served from 8am giving them nearly enough time to get the requisite eight hours sleep. They were both billeted in the Lakeside building so were able to support each other against the effects of two glasses of wine as they wobbled their way back. When they reached the foyer Dora whispered, respectful of those who might already be asleep, "Shall we meet here at 7.45 and face breakfast together?"

Stifling a yawn, Erica nodded in agreement "Lovely - see you in the morning and thanks for a great evening."

. . .

'Tomorrow is a new day with no mistakes in it,' Erica told herself, quoting from Anne of Green Gables. She often motivated her students with it when they'd had a bad day. She sincerely hoped that it would remain that way as she drifted off to sleep.

Chapter 8

Sunday 6th August 2023

It took Erica a moment to remember where she was as her alarm interrupted her slumber at 7am. She lazily rolled over and nestled into the crisp clean sheets and pillowcase for one last minute before forcing herself to put the kettle on for her morning cuppa. Considering the late night and consumption of wine, she had slept like a log. She was, however, feeling troubled by a dream. As with most dreams, she could not recall the finer details. It had been peculiar and, although it made perfect sense at the time, she could not make sense of it as she dutifully closed the bathroom door and took a quick shower.

'The fire alarm had gone off in the middle of the night and it had been her fault for showering without closing the door. Everyone had gathered in the corridor where she had joined them wearing a moose onesie. The fire service had arrived but there was no fire. She was frog marched into a room to be interrogated by a fire chief who looked incredibly like Richard Noyles. She couldn't explain why she was wearing a moose onesie and he just kept laughing at her.'

. . .

She now had an irrational dislike for Richard Noyles which was tormenting her as she rough dried her hair and drank her cup of tea. Why did I have to bump into him yesterday, she bewailed to herself as she rushed to dress and apply some make up.

Gathering her thoughts and backpack, Erica hurried to the foyer arriving just ahead of Dora. It was a bright sunny morning, and they admired the colourful blooms in the formal flower beds of the landscaped gardens as they ambled to the dining hall.

"Why is the smell of bacon so enticing?" Dora queried.

"One of life's delights and unsolved mysteries." Erica responded as they joined the breakfast queue.

Breakfast proved to be less traumatic than dinner, passing off without incident. It was much more relaxing having Dora to chat to and they agreed to catch up in the bar area at the next coffee break. Parting company, Erica opted to sit outside on one of the picnic tables and benches where she studied the timetable in the morning sunshine. Looking at her notebook she was reminded to look up the meaning of her name, so she took out her phone to search. Google obliged.

'The feminine version of Eric derived from the Old Norse meaning "eternal ruler" or "ever powerful". The Latin word for Heather, a long-lasting plant deriving from the Ericaceae family. The name Erica embodies the themes of "influence and endurance" qualities that provide "motivation and comfort" throughout their life.'

. . .

Erica could not help feeling deflated. Nothing could be further from reality, and she was disappointed at her findings. It would take a lot of thought to link herself to the meaning of her name. She could not see herself writing any inspirational poetry based on it. Attempting to lift her spirits, she reminded herself that she wasn't really interested in becoming a poet and she would be late for her first session if she sat there much longer. People were making their way to the various meeting rooms, and she hurried across to the main lecture hall.

Glenda Allot was delivering a specialist talk entitled '*From Novice to Novelist – how to write your first novel*', which seemed a sensible place for Erica to begin. She found a seat and settled in. The first hour flew by as they discussed writing a synopsis, blurb, and opening chapter. Erica was feeling inspired as they broke for refreshments. She dashed down the corridor to the bar area where she waited patiently at one of the drink stations to grab a cup of tea.

As promised, Dora arrived, and they opted to sit in the Vinery to have their refreshments. It was bright, airy, and calm. Erica took the opportunity to take a selfie with Carla and Dora, capturing the gardens in the background. She was just about to line up a shot of Carla, apparently drinking from the mug, when Erica spotted Richard who was striding towards their table. She instinctively grabbed the toy in an unsuccessful attempt to hide it but in doing so sent the mug of tea flying from the table, across the floor to the feet of an unsuspecting Richard.

"Missed! It seems as though you're out to get me one way or

another," he responded as he checked his tanned legs and white trainers for any fall out.

Erica could not gauge his mood. "I'm so sorry," she spluttered, jumping up "did it hit you?" Cautiously, she moved towards him with a paper serviette clasped in her hand as if to help.

"Can't see any damage so you're off the hook this time," he replied with a withering look. "I was just coming to confirm our one-to-one session. I have you down for 2pm tomorrow in the lounge - if I survive that long." He looked questioningly at Erica who was surreptitiously trying to stuff Carla back into the rucksack.

"Yes thanks," she replied as Richard turned to leave. "So sorry – how embarrassing. See you tomorrow."

Dora was stifling a laugh as Erica tried to regain her composure and mop up the dregs of tea with the paper serviette. "No wonder you're still single if that's how you treat men," she teased once the *target* had departed. "I thought you were going to rub his gorgeous *'pins'* with that," she continued nodding towards the serviette.

"I don't know what's the matter with me," Erica complained. "Of all the people - I have to keep running into him! Do you think he saw Carla? He must think I'm an absolute fruitcake and I've got to have a serious conversation with him tomorrow! So much for Anne of Green Gables"

"Don't worry, he probably didn't notice anything." Dora tried to reassure her with a comforting arm around the shoulder as they hurried back to their respective sessions.

"What's it got to do with Anne of Green Gables?" she added perplexed.

"Just a quote – I'll explain another time," Erica responded hastily.

"See you at lunch," she called as Erica turned into the main lecture hall. It was time for part two of Glenda Allot's '*From Novice to Novelist*'.

The tea incident had unnerved Erica and she was finding it harder to concentrate. She was relieved that Glenda's notes would be made available after the Summer School had ended as she was struggling to write everything down. She decided to just sit back and listen, hoping that something would be absorbed by her buzzing brain. As the session drew to a close, she glanced at the timetable. Erica's heart sank when she realised that the first afternoon workshop was being led by Richard Noyles. It was billed as a 'not to be missed' workshop for budding crime writers who wish to use forensics in their novels. This was of obvious use to her for her own novel, so she felt compelled to attend. 'If only it was later in the week,' she thought despondently.

Erica exited the hall and felt butterflies fluttering in the pit of her stomach as she made her way to meet Dora for lunch. Let's hope I don't embarrass myself again, she worried as she joined Dora in the lunch queue. "I'm not sure I can face a whole session with Richard Noyles this afternoon," she whispered to Dora as they waited to be served.

During lunch, Dora persuaded Erica to accompany her to '*Forensics – Making it Real in Crime Writing*' which was being held in the meeting room described as Butterly 1 in the timetable. They agreed to rendezvous just before 2.15pm. This gave Erica an hour to relax so she took a stroll around the lake before returning to her room to prepare for the afternoon's session with Richard. She decided to leave Carla in her room for the rest of the day and just drink water in the hope of averting any further issues. She placed Carla on the dressing table, slotted her water bottle into the side pouch of her rucksack, and set off to meet Dora.

Erica cursed to herself on arriving at Butterly 1 as it was apparent that the session was very popular. This resulted in her having to sit with Dora in the front row or endure standing up for a whole hour at the back. Dora nudged her forward to the only vacant seats and she sulkily took her place with ten minutes to spare. It was another warm day, and she could feel herself flushing despite wearing her coolest, loosest dress. Is it the heat or just stupid nerves she thought, closing her eyes, and trying to slow her breathing. She anticipated the arrival of the 'star of the show', Richard Noyles. Why she was being so sarcastic in her head, she did not know. With her eyes still closed, she was envisaging a fanfare with a grand announcement and Richard strutting in wearing a gold sequinned cape.

Erica was close to dozing off when Dora nudged her gently. Richard had walked in and was quickly finishing his preparations. She noted that he had exchanged his shorts for a light-coloured pair of chinos. A loose, white, linen shirt with the sleeves rolled to his elbows emphasised his tanned face and arms. With his brown leather sandals, and designer aviator sunglasses he would not have looked out of place on a tropical beach advertising Winter Sun holidays, she imagined.

. . .

He really is messing with my head, Erica thought as she tried to look inconspicuous amongst the sea of faces looking at Richard. She clutched her notebook and pen waiting for the show to begin and took a quick swig from her water bottle.

Richard glanced at his watch while using his left hand to remove the sunglasses from his head to lay them on the table. He picked up a pen before proceeding to introduce himself to the crowded room. "Hi everyone and welcome to this afternoon's workshop. Thank you all for coming. It's always a bit disconcerting to see so many people who are anxious to learn how to kill someone without leaving a trace." He smiled and paused as the captivated audience collectively chuckled on cue. Erica subconsciously rolled her eyes and glanced at Dora who was transfixed and laughing with the crowd.

Erica was not surprised to learn that Richard had grown up in '*The North*' due to his accent. She was intrigued to learn that he was born and raised in leafy Wilmslow, Cheshire, in a stable middle class family; had attended a comprehensive school where he had achieved average grades at A Level before joining the Greater Manchester Police in 2006. He had spent five years in the Greater Manchester Force before transferring to Staffordshire Police in 2011. He worked as a detective constable in their drugs and murder squads for the next six years. Due to undisclosed personal reasons, which generated untold curiosity for Erica, he had left the police and moved south to Bristol in 2017, where he currently lived with his long-haired German Shepherd named Boris. He had begun his journey to publication during the lockdown periods of the COVID-19 pandemic. His first book, *'Life in the Fast Lane'* had been published in 2021 and his second book, *'How to get Away with Murder'*, had taken another year to complete. This had opened doors to earning an income as a speaker and tutor at various writing and writers' events around the country.

His short biography reassured Erica that he had the perfect background to provide realistic content for the revenge attack on her character. Temporarily distracted, a thought crossed her mind. I wonder who's looking after Boris while he's here. She scribbled a quick note to remind her to dig deeper and to read Richard's books.

Using his pen, Richard pointed and tapped at the individual words on his power point whilst informing the audience of the contents of his session. Erica tutted to herself as he tapped and spoke each word. Firearms, knives, and explosives all seemed an unlikely choice for her revenge, but poison and fire were a definite possibility she thought. As his talk progressed, Richard answered many of Erica's unspoken questions. Erica scribbled furiously ensuring that she had copious notes. There were so many things that she had to consider. How will Stacey dispose of the body? Where will she dispose of the body? Annoying that the school chemistry lab won't have large enough quantities of acid to emulate the Acid Bath Murders of Haigh. She mulled it over as Richard explained the many types of poison and the effects they have on the human body. Poison was definitely looking the favourite option as it was too complicated to obtain firearms and knives involved getting too close and personal. Disposing of a six-foot male weighing fourteen stone was going to need some careful planning as his corpse would be a dead weight to move and she did not fancy describing dismemberment. Maybe there's no need to dispose of him, she puzzled. It should look like an accident and there should be no forensic evidence left at the scene. She jotted down her thoughts for discussion later with Dora.

Weaving his pen through his fingers as he spoke, Richard had moved on to the subject of forensic evidence. Erica began to doubt that there was any way anyone could get away with murder in the twenty first century. DNA was a huge advancement in capturing perpetrators as are the proliferation of CCTV cameras on most streets and many domestic buildings. Something else to bear in mind she noted. Erica began to feel frustrated as there was so much more to creating the perfect murder. Frustration heightened her irritation at the pen fiddling and tapping as Richard moved on to the handling of crime scenes and the importance of correct terminology. He concluded by reminding everyone that, *"In the UK, bodies are taken to the mortuary and undergo a post-mortem. They don't go to the morgue for an autopsy."*

Polite applause rippled around the room.

Erica was starting to wilt in the heat and reached down for her water bottle. Taking a large gulp, she attempted to discreetly check the time on her watch as she raised the bottle to her lips. Much to her relief, the hour was nearly up, so she could get some fresh air.

. . .

She could have sworn that Richard looked directly at her as he drew the session to a close by asking if anyone had any questions before they broke for afternoon tea. Predictably, there were plenty of questions from the attentive audience, but Erica decided to save hers for the one-to-one session the next day. Finally, the last question was answered, and she was able to escape with Dora out into the sunshine.

Tea in hand, Erica and Dora adjourned to a picnic bench in the gardens to debrief. Erica retrieved her notebook and noticed that the only question she had jotted down was:

1. *Who is looking after Boris?*

She hastily added a couple of other queries:

2. *Why did Richard leave the police and move to Bristol?*
3. *What did he do on leaving the police?*

As an afterthought she scribbled:

4. *Why do I need to know?*

Dora looked over Erica's shoulder at the notes. "Oh, I can answer number two and three" she proudly offered.

"Richard Noyles left the police after his long-term girlfriend had been killed on a zebra crossing by a speeding driver who was under the influence of drugs. He struggled to come to terms with her death and left the police on medical grounds. He was also disillusioned by the justice system as the driver was convicted but given a very short sentence. He became a speed awareness instructor in Bristol to try and educate the public on the danger of speeding. He eventually gave it up as it was a constant reminder of his loss."

Incredulous, Erica asked "How do you know all this?"

"I live in Bristol, and I've read his book, *'Life in the Fast Lane'*" she confirmed. "Of course, Richard Noyles is his nom de plume," she added for dramatic effect.

"What's his real name then?"

"It's an anagram of his real name, Nicholas Ryder."

Erica felt the blood drain from her entire body and was grateful that she was already sitting down as Dora threw this grenade in the room.

"But he looks nothing like Annoying Nick," Erica blurted out taking Dora by surprise.

"Who's Annoying Nick?" Dora queried whilst trying to make sense of Erica's reaction.

Erica took some deep breathes to try and prevent herself from passing out. She then explained to Dora about her brief but memorable encounter with Nicholas Ryder on her speed awareness course in November 2019. "I can't stand the bloke."

Erica was having trouble reconciling how she seemed to be attracted to Richard Noyles but couldn't stand Annoying Nick.

Things were beginning to make sense. His outward appearance was obviously quite different but there were other characteristics that had not changed. He wore his watch on his right wrist; his accent; the annoying tapping of his pen, and the weaving of his pen through his fingers as he spoke, were all still there. She wondered how she hadn't spotted the clues.

. . .

"So, he did remember my name and it wasn't my name badge that gave it away," she suggested to Dora who was struggling to take in the revelations. "That was just before lockdown four years ago and he still remembers me!" she exclaimed. "He must hate my guts as well as thinking that I'm a prize fruitcake" she added.

"Well, that should only matter if you're harbouring desires for him," Dora proffered, trying to elicit where this was leading.

"I'm so confused," Erica moaned, unsure if Dora was making a statement or asking a question. She certainly did not know the answer and wanted the ground to open up and swallow her.

They both sipped their tea which, by this time, was nearly cold, and sat in awkward silence for what seemed an eternity. Dora eventually broke the silence and suggested that they go for a stroll around the lake to gather their thoughts. They abandoned their tea and set off towards the lake in the hope of some divine inspiration.

"I'm not sure I can meet him for the one to one tomorrow! Why is life always so complicated?" she wailed at Dora once they were out of earshot of other delegates.

"Don't be daft. You've got to go. It's obvious that you fancy the pants off him and even if you don't, he's the perfect person to help you finish your book," instructed Dora as she put a caring arm around Erica's slouching shoulders. "Anyway, you've paid a lot of money to be here, and it would be an absolute waste on a number of fronts if you didn't take advantage of the situation. He probably doesn't know that you know who he is either." She guided Erica slowly around the lake to a vacant bench.

. . .

Quietly they sat together, watching, and listening to the wildlife of the lake. Outwardly all was calm and still but inside Erica's head thoughts were spinning wildly. She was having trouble organising her emotions when Dora broke the silence. "Good grief, is that the time already?" She glanced at her watch. "It's 5.30pm! We're too late for 'Relax Your Mind'."

"What a shame," replied Erica , unconvincingly. "I could do with someone unwinding mine!"

Grabbing Erica's arm Dora encouraged her to stand, "Come on let's go and get ready for dinner and then we can have a drink in the bar." Obediently, Erica got to her feet, and they wandered lazily back to Lakeside to prepare for the evening.

As she dropped onto her bed, Erica wondered what else could happen to throw her off course.

Chapter 9

Main House Room 54

Nicholas Ryder was relaxing in his room on the first floor of the old house after his *'Forensics – Making it real in Crime Writing'* session. He was savouring a large mug of coffee while reflecting on the workshop before getting ready for dinner. Seeing Erica sitting in the front row had made him nervous especially since his recent encounters with her on arriving at Swanwick. He had hoped that she did not inadvertently *'attack'* him while he was in mid flow and was relieved that the whole session had passed off without any embarrassing incidents. He was trying to come to terms with the coincidence of her turning up on this course after their first encounter on the speed awareness course four years earlier. He had deliberately failed to mention his previous job as a speed awareness instructor in his opening biography when he saw her in the room. He had noticed her roll her eyes when he made his introduction. He sat back with his mug in hand and closed his eyes to try and recall their first meeting on 6th November 2019.

He had not been in a very good frame of mind that day in November as it was the second anniversary of the accident that killed Chloe. He was still blaming himself for the fact that she had jumped out of his car and stormed off. They had been arguing again. The relationship had been going through a rough patch and she had seized the opportunity to leave the car as they stopped at a red light. Stubbornly, he had driven on without looking back and did not see the impact of the car hitting her on the zebra crossing a few minutes later. He could, however, vividly remember his colleagues from the police station calling on him and breaking the news of her death. She had been mown down by a young man who was speeding and under the influence of drugs. He had failed to stop but was caught, arrested, and eventually faced prosecution.

Nick had spent months going through the torture of *'if only'* and would have gone completely mad had it not been for Mike, his counsellor. Mike had gradually helped him to the realisation that his relationship with Chloe had run its course months before the incident that permanently ended it. They both wanted different things from their lives. He was keen to start a family and she was adamant that she didn't. He had wanted to progress within the Police Force, but she didn't want to move from her parents who lived close by. Little things had started to irritate him about her and vice versa. It had taken over two years for it to be acceptable to him to admit that they had fallen out of love. It had taken even longer for him to accept that it was not his fault that she had died and that it was normal for him to be grieving despite the relationship being near its end. She had, after all been a large part of his life and he didn't wish her any harm.

Despite the counselling, he had finally taken the decision to resign from the police. Disillusioned with the justice system that sent the offender to prison for only ten years for murdering the person that he thought he loved, he did not see the point in continuing.

Why the hell did I think that spending every day with idiots who speed would help me recover, he thought.

All of these feelings resurfaced every year, on 6th November, although thankfully now they were less intense. Unfortunately for the candidates on the 6th of November 2019, he was not at his best, he thought.

He recalled looking out of the staff room window and observing a young woman taking photos of a toy animal that was sitting on the wall in front of the building. "What the hell is she up to?" he had asked his colleagues who all rushed to observe the incident. "Maybe she's taken a wrong turn and is looking for the nursery down the road," laughed his colleague. "Nope, she's heading for the front door," he had confirmed to the audience at the back of the room. "Just my luck I'll have her in my class this morning," he had complained to anyone who was listening before making his way to the classroom. He had found the toy Llama on the floor as he made his way across the hallway. With hindsight, he should have discreetly given it back to its owner but instead he had shamefully held it up in front of everyone for them to claim it back causing maximum embarrassment. This was his first encounter with Miss Erica Mills who had been caught travelling at fifty-eight miles per hour in a fifty mile per hour zone. If he remembered correctly, she already had at least six points on her licence. How come I can remember that much detail and struggle to remember what I did yesterday. *'You forget what you want to remember, and remember what you want to forget,'* he thought recalling *The Road* by Cormac McCarthy.

He had been on a mission to educate the *'morons'* who thought it was ok to speed and on that day, they were going to heed his lesson.

He had become adept at countering drivers who tried to justify their need for speed, and he always had the upper hand as it was his decision if they left the course without the penalty points on their licences.

Erica had been unusual compared to the majority of disinterested parties who attended the courses. She appeared nervous and quiet to begin with especially after the Llama toy incident. He had been shocked when she had answered back at him when he made the opening statement about leaving five minutes earlier rather than speeding. He had been close to kicking her off the course at the first hurdle. With hindsight, perhaps it was just the sign of a sense of humour combined with nerves that ordinarily would have been innocent. Unfortunately for Erica, he was not in the mood for humour or nerves on that particular day.

He had continued with the usual course content before noticing that Erica was either asleep or in a trance. He had deliberately put her on the spot with a question about towing caravans. It had obviously taken a few seconds for her to return to reality as she had caused the room some amusement when she had blurted out that she did not have a caravan and never would. She must have been mortified, he thought, with a tinge of regret at being insensitive. Looking back, he could see that it possibly was amusing, but at the time he was developing a major dislike for the eccentric, scatty and disinterested Erica. He could not abide anyone who did not share his passionate hatred for anyone who thought speeding was acceptable. This was always intensified on the anniversary of his loss.

With the onset of Covid – 19, in 2020, he had made the decision to quit his instructor role as it was a constant reminder of that November day. He was persuaded by a close friend to attempt to write a book about his experiences in the police and his reasons for leaving. This had led to the publication of *'Life in The Fast Lane'* which had made him a few pounds.

He couldn't watch a TV Crime show or read a crime thriller

without picking fault with the portrayal of crime scene investigations and police methods. He had then tried his hand at using his knowledge to help crime writers get the science correct by writing his second publication, *'How to get Away with Murder'*. It had turned out to be a very popular subject and he had begun to attend various writing and writers' events before finally having the courage to become a subject matter expert in his own right.

Being shut away during the *'lockdowns'* had suited him. He had re invented himself as Richard Noyles the author and subsequent lecturer. He was quietly proud of the anagram of his given name. Boris, his loyal German Shepherd, had kept him company and ensured that he stayed fit and sane during this period. He had allowed his hair to grow and a beard to develop to the point that he sometimes did not recognise himself when he caught his reflection. He had remained single and had no desire to pursue a new relationship.

Taking a gulp of his rapidly cooling coffee, he thought about his more recent encounters with Erica. Four years on and he had observed that the toy Llama was now being photographed in various locations around the campus. It was a complete puzzle to him why she always seemed to carry this toy with her. Maybe I can bring that up at our one to one tomorrow, he thought as he drained the last of his coffee.

Then there was the first occasion when she had bumped into him at the bar. He tried to remember if he had called her by her name. If he had, she must have wondered how he knew it so soon. Hopefully she didn't notice or put it down to her name badge, he assured himself. He had then deliberately sat opposite her when he saw her rucksack hanging on the back of the chair on the first dinnertime. It had been obvious to him that she was nervous and uncomfortable at his presence which frustrated him. When her phone rang, Erica had been oblivious to the fact that it had been possible to hear the caller from across the table. He was still amused at the fact she had used a junk phone call to make her escape and found himself smiling.

He was a cat toying with a mouse. He hoped that Erica was unaware that he was deliberately picking his moments to appear. He had nearly paid the price when she upset the mug of tea whilst trying to hide the Llama from him in the Vinery. His pristine white trainers only just avoided being speckled with tea drops as the mug flew from the table. He had been amused as she had approached him with paper napkins in an effort to mop up. Part of him regretted that she had not used them to dry his bare legs.

Catching sight of his phone screen, he realised that he was running out of time to prepare for dinner. He hastily took a shower before assuming the persona of Richard Noyles and heading for the dining hall.

As he walked down the stairs and along the corridors, he deliberated if he was looking forward to the private meeting with Erica, but curiosity was his overriding emotion.

Erica met Dora for a much-needed drink in the bar prior to heading into the dining hall. They were just standing up to make their way to the queue when, with impeccable timing, Richard Noyles marched around the corner and almost collided with them. Apologising profusely, he addressed Erica, "Glad I've bumped into you," he smiled "Don't suppose you could email your manuscript to me before tomorrow's meeting so that I can get an idea of what we're going to be talking about?" he asked, handing her a business card from his jacket pocket. "The email address is on this" he said as he thrust the card into her hand.

"Will do," she managed as he continued purposefully towards the dining queue.

Erica and Dora followed at a more sedate pace and took their place further back. Whilst waiting, Erica used her phone to email her manuscript to Richard so that she did not forget to do it later after a few drinks in the bar.

Erica had just hit the send button when it dawned on her that she hadn't changed the name of her character from *'Dick'*. "Hopefully, Richard has a sense of humour," Dora suggested trying to calm her down. "And anyway, it's not his real name so he shouldn't take offence," she added hurriedly in an attempt to smooth over the situation. Erica was mortified once again and wanted to curl up and die in the corner.

Her mind was taken off her mistake by the pressing need to decide what she wanted to eat. They both opted for chicken casserole and vegetables which they agreed was the lesser of two evils and washed it down with an Eton Mess for pudding.

Having refuelled, Dora opted to attend the Open Mic Poetry at 8pm but could not persuade Erica to do the same. Erica wanted to take the opportunity to talk with Lucy and download *'Life in the Fast Lane'* onto her Kindle. They both agreed to catch up later in the bar at 9.30pm.

It was a relief to Erica to be in the peace and tranquillity of her room. Nice as Dora was, Erica just needed her own space with time to reflect. Plumping up the pillows she arranged them so that she could comfortably sit up on the bed with a cup of tea to text Lucy. For the first time in their friendship, they abandoned texting after ten minutes. They both concluded it would take too long to text everything that had been happening since Erica's arrival at Swanwick and agreed to talk it through.

Predictably, Lucy enthusiastically encouraged Erica to *'reel him in'*. The only trouble was that Erica was not the type who did *'reeling in'*. Lucy had Googled Richard Noyles and was in no doubt that he was worth pursuing.

Erica filled her in on the fact that he was actually *'Annoying Nick'* which was making it difficult for her to totally commit to the possibility of any kind of relationship, should it present itself.

"That was four years ago and he's Richard now not Nick" countered Lucy using her own unique logic. "And he's got a gorgeous dog," Lucy announced as if that was a deciding factor.

"It might be a mangy mutt for all we know," retorted Erica "We've not seen it," she added for clarity.

"He doesn't look like the sort of guy to have a horrid dog," Lucy added annoyed at Erica's negativity.

"Anyway, he probably thinks I'm a prize fruitcake after all the things that have happened so far, so I don't know why we're even having this conversation now," Erica added sulkily. "Based on past experiences I hardly dare consider the possibility that someone like Richard or Nick or whoever he is, would even look at me twice. We don't even know if he's single," she added sinking further into despondency.

Erica could not recall if she had seen him wearing a ring and made a mental note to add it to discovering who was looking after Boris the dog.

"You've got to be in it to win it," Lucy cheerfully countered. "And you're certainly in it at the moment. Let me know how it goes tomorrow and don't keep me in suspense."

Erica promised to call Lucy as soon as she could before hanging up.

Erica's phone pinged with a final message from Lucy. *'Go girl, you can do it! Heart emoji XX'*

Erica responded, *'Thanks, heart emoji, XX, but I can't stand him!'*

'Don't be an arse,' was Lucy's final response on the matter

and Erica conceded defeat for the time being with a '*Thumbs up*' emoji.

The catch up with Lucy had taken far longer than Erica had anticipated but she still had time to download the book to her Kindle. She felt unexplained nervous excitement as she waited for the book to appear in her Kindle library. She was about to pry into the life of Richard Noyles, but her curiosity was too strong to ignore the opportunity.

Finally, after what seemed like an eternity, the book was safely stored in her Kindle library. She scanned through the prologue before reluctantly closing her device and leaving it on charge. She had ten minutes before her rendezvous with Dora in the bar and she didn't want to miss out on getting a seat. She hastily reapplied her lipstick and double checked her appearance in the mirror before grabbing her bag and heading towards the bar.

Chapter 10

Main House Room 54

On the other side of the campus, Richard Noyles was taking advantage of an evening off. He had noticed the arrival of the manuscript email from Erica during dinner and felt a strong compulsion to read its content. Back in his room he kicked off his leather sandals before locating one of the hidden bottles of wine that he had smuggled onto the premises. Despite reading that it was forbidden to bring alcohol or food into the rooms on the grounds of health and safety, he had hidden four bottles of red wine in his wardrobe. Using his knowledge of the law, he decided that the food and drink police, and the Health and Safety Executive, would have difficulty prosecuting him or proving his guilt. Defiantly, he poured himself a glass of wine and opened up his MacBook Pro. Taking a hearty sip from his contraband, he opened the file from Erica and began reading.

From the opening sentence to the end of chapter one he had been hooked. He double checked that he was actually reading Erica's work. It definitely was from Erica.

How can she write with such insight and accuracy, he

thought as he read the first two chapters. His own knowledge of the drug scene from policing in the Staffordshire drug squad had provided him with the ability to judge her work for authenticity.

Dumbfounded, he began to suspect that much of what was being written about was based on personal experience. It was far too authentic to have been dreamt up by someone as timid as Erica he thought.

For the next couple of hours, he was engrossed until the story ground to halt. Erica had written some notes to herself. '*Need to plot a sensible revenge/kill him off*' and '*hero needs to be invented*'.

Richard began to suspect that there was far more to Erica than met the eye and that life had not been a bed of roses. He was concerned that their meeting tomorrow would be awkward. He hoped that she was not in need of therapy rather than a writing coach. Who am I to talk, he questioned, recalling his own vulnerabilities. One thing was certain: she was very good at writing. The second thing that was certain was that he felt compelled to help her '*kill off*' the '*thieving rat*'. Anyone linked to the drug scene always evoked an intense feeling of hatred. It's unfortunate that she's chosen to name him *Dick* though, he thought, unable to decide if he was amused or insulted.

Richard took out his notepad and wrote a few prompts for their meeting. He had been reminded of an unsolved murder case involving the death of a junky so perhaps they could use that to come up with a suitable ending for '*Dick*'.

God, I hope she doesn't refer to me as '*Dick*,' he thought as he'd guessed why she'd chosen the name. It also made him even more certain that she was writing from personal experience. He felt quietly confident, due to the fact that she wanted help, that her experience hadn't included bumping off the offending villain. (Or so he hoped).

Time was flying but his brain could not switch off from trying to murder Erica's past. He was no psychiatrist, but he could sense that Erica would benefit from a literary closure of this story. I'll not be surprised if she's still single, he thought sympathetically which took him off guard.

It was well after midnight by the time he closed his computer and notebook. He had barely touched his illicit drink, so he poured the contents back into the bottle and hid it away for another evening.

As he drifted off to sleep, he was uncertain if he was truly ready to officially meet 'Stacey'.

Chapter 11

Monday 7th August 2023

Erica woke early to another sunny morning. It was Monday and her appointment with Richard Noyles loomed on the horizon. She decided to have a lazy morning and relax in the sunshine after having breakfast with Dora. They had arranged to meet at 8am so she had a long shower before finding something suitable to wear. She opted for a pink floral maxi dress with short puff sleeves and a comfortable pair of white Converse shoes. It was already too warm to bother with a cardigan which pleased her as she was less likely to lose it and it was one thing less to carry. She filled her water bottle, grabbed her Kindle, and added them to her rucksack before strolling to meet her friend in the foyer of the Lakeside.

As Dora devoured her full English breakfast, Erica pushed her scrambled eggs around the plate. She was unusually disinterested in her breakfast and struggled to eat the toast and eggs before her. Dora winked at her and smiled as she polished off her last piece of toast. "What's up with you this morning?" she asked pretending not to have a clue. "Are you off your oats?" she added. "I didn't think we had that heavy a sesh last night." Dora was starting to irritate Erica who was not in the mood for the friendly banter. She was annoyed with herself for feeling so nervous and tried to counter the feeling by taking some deep breaths. It didn't work. She finally responded, "I just need some fresh air, that's all. It's too hot in here."

"Are you coming to Evelyn Napier's *'Competition Tips and Tricks' workshop?'*" asked Dora enthusiastically.

Erica paused to consider her response as she didn't want to offend her friend. "No thanks, I thought I would find a quiet, shady spot and do some reading and research before my meeting this afternoon if you don't mind. Perhaps we could meet at coffee break?"

Dora tried to disguise her feelings, but Erica could tell she was disappointed. Erica suggested they should exchange phone numbers in case of any unexpected change of plans. Dora agreed. They parted company and went about their own business with the understanding they could easily contact each other should the need arise.

Erica chose a shaded bench as far away from civilisation as she could and made herself comfortable. She began reading *'Life in the Fast Lane'* as swiftly as she could. She was hungry to devour every word as soon as she could as she felt it contained information she needed about the curiosity that was Nick Ryder aka Richard Noyles.

Dora had been correct when she had regaled her with the story of his girlfriend being killed by a drug fuelled young man who was speeding. As he poured his heart out on the pages in front of her she struggled to continue reading as her eyes blurred with tears. No wonder he had a passionate dislike for morons like her, she thought reflecting on her experience in November 2019. As she continued reading it became apparent the date of her speed awareness course must have been the anniversary of Chloe's death. It seemed unsettling to Erica to now know the name of the person who had been Nick's raison d'être. She wondered again about who was looking after Boris. She also wondered who would stand a chance of breaking through the pain barrier of such a traumatic end to a relationship. Slowly Erica realised that she was talking her way out of any possibility of 'reeling him in' as Lucy had put it yesterday. From what she was reading, Chloe would be a hard act to follow if not an impossible one. One thing was certain. Her opinion of Nick Ryder was improving the more she read.

Despite being in the shade, Erica was beginning to swelter in the heat of the day. Her water bottle was nearly empty, and she needed to stretch her legs. It was almost time for the workshops to spill out, so she dashed across the manicured lawns to the bar. She had hopes of being near the front of the queue for the hot water machine. As she entered the bar there were a handful of delegates milling around chatting, so she grabbed a tea bag and headed for the hot water machine and some milk. Much to her amusement, there was a sign above the milk dispenser advising, 'This may contain milk,' under a picture of a cow. Obviously, there must be some people who need this level of advice she thought as she smiled to herself.

Depositing her tea bag in the appropriate receptacle, Erica turned to locate Dora and a seat. As she approached the Vinery, Richard appeared beside her. It was enough to make her jump out of her skin, but she thankfully held on to her tea without throwing it at him for the second time in two days.

. . .

"See you this afternoon Erica." He smiled. "Just wondering if you fancy meeting in the grounds rather than the stuffy lounge?"

"Fine by me." She managed a smile which she hoped hadn't looked like a grimace. "Where shall we meet?"

Richard pointed towards the window and a wooden picnic table and bench seats. They were in a secluded position on the lawn offering privacy and shade.

"See you there at two," he added before leaving as quickly as he had arrived.

"Why are you so flustered?" asked Dora as Erica gingerly placed her mug of tea on the table. Erica pulled out a chair and gently lowered herself onto the cushion before updating Dora on Richard's near miss with the mug of tea again.

"He caught me by surprise, and I was this close to chucking the whole thing over him." Erica indicated with her thumb and index finger the closeness of the incident.

Dora laughed. "He'll be lucky to survive the week at this rate. I can't wait to hear all about your meeting, if you both survive. See you at dinner." Dora got up leaving Erica to finish her tea and top up her water bottle.

Erica returned to her shaded bench to continue quenching her thirst for information about Richard Noyles. She opened her kindle which obligingly resumed where she had left off. The following chapters revealed how he had struggled with guilt and depression as he tried to come to terms with the death of Chloe. Erica snapped her kindle shut and shoved it into her bag. There didn't seem much point in her developing feelings for the man with two names as it was unlikely he would ever recover from his loss. She could not face reading any more. At least the book provided an excuse for his demeanour when he'd delivered the speed awareness session. Feeling deflated, Erica grabbed her belongings and retired to her room to regroup. She resigned herself to the fact that Richard was never going to be interested in her and she did not want to play second fiddle to his one and only love. A feeling of calm washed over her, and for the first time she felt relaxed.

She only had an hour to grab some lunch and prepare before her meeting with Richard. As she trotted to the dining hall, she felt liberated and free knowing that it was business as usual regarding affairs of the heart. She was a better actress than she thought.

Richard was prepared and waiting for Erica as she crossed the lawn to the agreed meeting point. His laptop was open, and he had a notepad and pen beside it. Erica tried to look cheery as she arrived and took her place opposite him. They exchanged pleasantries as she extracted her laptop from her rucksack and mirrored his set up with her own notebook and pen.

It became clear to her that he had read the manuscript as he began to talk through the synopsis. Erica hoped that she wasn't blushing as he complimented her on the detailed descriptions and highly accurate portrayal of a person involved in the drug scene. He seemed almost as keen as she was to exact revenge on the antagonist. She surmised this was due to the fact that Chloe had been killed by someone high on drugs. She wasn't sure if she should bring it into the conversation, so she let it pass, for now. Maybe further down the line it would be appropriate when they were more comfortable in each other's company she thought.

Richard was glancing through his notes and twiddling his pen through his fingers. Erica tried not to let it annoy her as she anticipated his next comment.

"Your story made me think of a case that I was working on for Staffordshire police. I was called to a scene where a young lad had been found dead on some waste ground near to his flat. It had all the hallmarks of a drug deal gone wrong and there was no evidence to work with except a gold chain found at the scene. They never found his phone and couldn't trace anything about it. It must have been a burner phone."

"How was he killed?" she asked. "Is it something I could use in my plot?"

"It appeared that he had been bludgeoned with a blunt, heavy object. My guess would be a baseball bat."

"Weren't there any other clues to work on like DNA or CCTV or anything?" Erica was intrigued and hopeful that she could find a way for Stacy to get away with murder.

"No. We scoured local CCTV for anything suspicious but there was no coverage at the actual scene. It was just out of sight of the camera covering the car park."

"I don't suppose the police were that bothered about solving it if he was a druggy?" she asked.

"Oh, they were. But more for the family than anything else."

"Surely they'd want to get the drug dealers off the streets too?" she questioned.

"Sadly, the perpetrators would only be the foot soldiers and well down the supply chain. Mr Big wouldn't get his own hands dirty. They wouldn't ever talk, even if they knew who had ordered the hit. If they did grass, they would end up dead themselves. Being in prison wouldn't protect them."

"That's so awful." Erica sighed.

"Anyway, that was nearly ten years ago and nothing much has changed in Stoke since then as far as I know. The likes of Dean Scott are two a penny," he added as he glanced back at his notes.

Erica did a swift calculation. 'Nearly ten years ago' would have been 2014; Stoke is short for Stoke on Trent, and Dean Scott, although a common name, most likely was the person known to her as Dee. Her mind raced at supersonic speed as she processed the potential coincidence and she felt herself become nauseous and lightheaded.

Taking a deep breath she asked, "What sort of gold chain did they find?"

"If I remember rightly, it was a St Christopher."

Richard looked bemused as Erica thrust her belongings into her rucksack.

"So sorry I don't feel well," she managed before charging off across the lawn towards the Lakeside accommodation block.

Her head was spinning, and she hoped that she was not going to spew all over the lawns. Other delegates were making their way to afternoon tea in the bar, and she swerved them as she rushed to the safety of her room.

Opening the door, she jammed the key card in the slot and dived into the bathroom. She relaxed allowing herself to finally regurgitate her lunch in private. Grabbing some tissue, she cleaned her face and washed the vile taste away from her mouth with a glass of water. She brushed her teeth with a double helping of toothpaste before checking her appearance in the mirror. Her face was blotchy and red but thankfully, she hadn't made a mess on the floor or her clothing. She felt compelled to take a shower and change her clothes.

As she showered, she went over the scenario of the death of a person called Dean Scott in Stoke on Trent in 2014. It could not be a coincidence. The only evidence at the scene was a gold St Christopher necklace. She wracked her brains trying to remember when she last saw Tom wearing his St Christopher but nothing specific came to mind. She tried to convince herself that although she wore hers all the time, Tom probably didn't. If he did it would likely be under his clothing and not visible. She recalled her conversation with Tom when she was trying to get him to help her with the plot to take revenge on *'Dick,'* the fictional Dean Scott. He had told her of his friends' eagerness to settle the score. She was sure that a baseball bat had been mentioned at some point in the discussions. Her head was still reeling as she dried her hair and tried to decide what to wear.

She finally settled on a pair of dark blue denim jeans and a floral print halter neck blouse. She was now far from feeling calm and relaxed. She needed to talk to someone but feared discussing any of it with Lucy or Dora.

. . .

She decided to text Tom.

'Just a random one. Have you still got the St Christopher that Mum gave you? X'

After a few agonising minutes Tom replied, *'Yes Why? X'*

'Send me a pic as I want to compare it to mine and show Dora X' she lied feebly.

'Can't find it atm. Laura must have moved it X'

'Have you lost it? X' she asked, dreading the answer.

'No I just can't find it. What's the big deal? X'

'It's not important but let me know if you find it. Mum will kill you if you can't!'

'Ok will do X'

She ended the dialogue with a *thumbs up* and *heart* emoji, followed by a *'X'*, which she hoped made it *sound* light-hearted.

Erica felt tears sliding down her cheeks as she tried to make sense of everything. She was overwhelmed by what she had just heard from Richard, and the potential enormity of it.

RICHARD! In all the turmoil she had not even thought about Richard. She had abandoned him mid-session without any explanation. Erica resigned herself to the fact that she had blown her chances of his help and that he would definitely view her as a major fruitcake now. To be honest, it was the least of her worries as she tried to process the situation.

Erica made a mug of tea and sat with her feet up on the bed to drink it. She checked her phone in the hope that Tom had sent her a text to confirm that he had found his necklace. There was no such message. Leaning back on her pillows she closed her eyes and breathed deeply. As hard as she tried, she could not block out the one thought that played over and over like a stuck record in her mind.

It was highly likely that the scumbag who had robbed her of her savings had been bludgeoned to death by Tom. She should have been dancing on his grave but instead she was worried sick about her brother.

Erica awoke with a start and grabbed her phone. It had announced the arrival of a text message which she hoped was from Tom. It was her O2 bill. More importantly, it was 6.15pm and she was supposed to be meeting Dora for dinner. The neglected mug of tea was still waiting patiently on the bedside table and was destined to follow the other cold teas down the sink. She smoothed down her blouse and retied her ponytail. To her relief, Erica's eyes were no longer puffy and red and the blotches on her face had faded. The thought of eating did not appeal but her duty to Dora forced her to collect her things and hurry to join the queue.

Dora looked at Erica with mock agitation and tapped her watch as she joined her in the queue. The smell of food assaulted Erica's sensitive nostrils as she tried to act as though nothing untoward had happened.

"I thought you'd abandoned me Erica," said Dora as they edged forward to the counter.

"So sorry, I fell asleep and lost track of time."

Dora nudged Erica playfully and winked.

"How was your session with Richard?"

Drawing on her best acting skills, Erica attempted to look nonchalant as she responded.

"Ok thanks – I'll tell you more about it later – in private."

"Can't wait. Sounds intriguing."

"Don't get your hopes up. I don't want to disappoint you," Erica warned as they finally got to the counter.

The offering of fish or cottage pie was not appealing to Erica. She settled on a bowl of leek and potato soup with two bread rolls which she deliberated over until Dora had finished her meal. She felt a bit better and joined Dora in consuming a slab of fruit sponge smothered in custard. The rush of carbs and sugar assisted in lifting her spirits and they chatted idly.

Erica patiently listened to Dora's account of her session at Evelyn Napier's *'Competition Tips and Tricks'* workshop. Dora was now inspired to write some short stories and submit them to various competitions.

Evelyn Napier and her publisher, Blond Pulse, were running their own competition for Swanwick crime writers to enter, and Dora enthused for several minutes, sharing the details with Erica.

"The winner gets to be published by them which would be an amazing achievement."

"You must enter," encouraged Erica as they scraped the last crumbs from their bowls. They rose to leave while Dora chatted on about her ideas for a short crime thriller.

Dora removed the timetable from her large, knitted bag and scanned it for the evening's itinerary.

"It's the *'prose open mic'* tonight if you fancy it or *'The Big Quiz'*. I think I'll got to the prose."

"I don't feel very sociable and could do with some time to myself. Let's meet in the bar at 9pm and I'll fill you in."

Dora reluctantly agreed and Erica walked down the concourse to the exit with a view to hiding away in her room until 9pm. As she pressed the button to activate the door, she spotted Richard striding across the lawn towards Lakeside. She did an impressive military about turn and scurried into the accessible toilet to hide. Once safely locked inside, she realised her mistake. She now had no idea where Richard was and still risked bumping into him if she ventured forth. No fool proof escape plan was forthcoming. Erica could now hear voices which seemed close. These were followed by a polite tap on the door. How long had she been deliberating for? She wasn't sure. Hastily she flushed the toilet to signal her imminent exit and, after a suitable interlude, activated the hand drier. She hoped it would authenticate her reason to be there by limping out of the door. What was I thinking of? she scolded herself as she resumed walking normally. Not all disabilities are visible, she reminded herself, embarrassed at her performance. Thankfully, no one had questioned her as she exited and the lady with the wheeled walker seemed happy enough despite the wait.

Glancing out at the gardens and towards the Lakeside, Erica exited the building and furtively made her way along the path towards the main hall and the Lakeside building beyond. She glanced into the main hall where she observed the technical team setting up for the evening's open mic event. There was no danger there. Approaching the entrance, she began ransacking her bag for the key card to gain access to the Lakeside. Why does it always disappear to the depths she moaned to herself as the door crept open, and a familiar voice addressed her. With nowhere to hide, she slowly lifted her gaze and locked eye contact with Richard.

"Erica, just the person I was looking for, are you ok? I think I deserve an explanation."

"I'm so sorry, really, I don't know what to say. I just felt sick and had to dash."

Erica lowered her eyes and wished the ground would swallow her. Richard bent his head in an attempt to resume eye contact.

"Was it something I said?"

"No. Well yes, I suppose it was, but I can't talk about it. Not here anyway. It's not your fault, it's mine."

"I think we should try again if you can face it? It's a shame to miss the opportunity to help you develop your novel, if you still wish."

"I didn't think you'd want to bother with me again after the way I behaved."

"Until I know the reason, I'm not going to judge you. Are you free tomorrow morning at 10am? We can meet in the same spot as earlier today if that's ok?"

Erica nodded whilst fighting to hold back her emotions. The last thing she expected was for annoying Nick to sound like he had a heart. She managed to squeeze out her response.

"Thanks, yes that would be lovely. Sorry again"

"No problem, see you tomorrow."

Richard walked briskly towards the main building leaving Erica to head back to her sanctuary. Had she just imagined it or had Richard placed his hand on her shoulder? He had, she assured herself. It was a very light touch but a touch just the same. Had she flinched like she normally would? She couldn't recall. I hope you did not, she scolded herself.

Erica convinced herself that she hadn't reacted badly to the reassuring touch of the man with two names and was relieved that he appeared to be erring on the side of sympathy rather than anger.

Safely back in her room, Erica decided to avoid lying on the bed and instead opted for the chair by the window. She manoeuvred it so she could put up her feet on the bed, but it was not comfortable enough to risk nodding off before going to meet Dora. On second thoughts, she decided to set her alarm just in case. She spent a quiet hour flicking through Facebook and Instagram whilst drinking a rare hot mug of tea. She was still awake when the alarm reminded her it was time to go and meet Dora in the bar.

Dora had secured a couple of seats at a table tucked away in a corner of the Vinery, so it took a moment for Erica to locate her. There were two large glasses of Malbec strategically placed for each of them. Dora obviously did not want to waste any time and was bursting with curiosity as Erica deliberately took her time to get settled.

"Well?" said Dora, leaning purposefully into Erica. "Spill the beans."

Erica took a hearty glug from her glass and recounted the details of the meeting. She omitted her suspicions about Tom but explained the scenario of the murder of her ex-boyfriend in 2014 in an apparent drug deal that had gone wrong. Dora's eyes were wide with disbelief, and she was unusually quiet as Erica continued to explain how she had felt physically sick and had dashed out of the meeting. Erica played to her audience of one who was gripped by the drama. Dora finally spoke up when Erica began to narrate the graphic details of how she only just made it to her bathroom before spewing up her lunch.

"Too much information! You can stop there, thanks." Dora cupped her glass, lost for words.

Erica smiled wryly, "I just wish I knew who'd done it so I can shake their hand. I also wish I knew how they did it so I can use it in my novel."

"They obviously got away with it as it wasn't ever solved so it would be ideal."

Dora found her voice and enthusiastically tried to come up with a possible *modus operandi* which would have avoided detection.

"Leave it with me and I'll see what I can come up with."

Talking to Dora had brightened Erica's mood and she temporarily forgot her concerns about her brother's possible involvement. Dora was amused to hear about the accessible toilet incident and teased Erica with a quiet rendition of *'Oh dear what can the matter be, Erica got stuck in the lavatory….'*. Erica confirmed that she had agreed to try to meet him again but omitted the hand on the shoulder, for now. Dora was excited enough. Updated, Dora agreed to change the subject while they put the world to rights and enjoyed their drinks.

All Erica had to do now was get through the next day without any emotional outbursts or incidents.

Chapter 12

Monday 7th August 2023 Keynsham, Bristol

Tom was in his office catching up on some paperwork when the text from Erica interrupted his calculations. He was attempting to reconcile a client's Self-Assessment Tax Return and company accounts and was happy for the distraction. He opened the message and felt his blood run cold when he saw her question, *'Just a random one. Have you still got the St Christopher that Mum gave you? X.'* A lot of water had passed under the bridge since the events of December 2014, and he didn't relish reliving them.

Tom had married Laura in 2016 and they had bought a house together near their old student house share. Tom had found relatively well-paid employment with a firm of accountants in Bristol and was hybrid working as a legacy of COVID-19. Laura was pregnant with their first child and looking forward to maternity leave from her job in the Bristol Children's hospital where she was a paediatric nurse. Being a Key worker she had been at the coal face when COVID struck but had been fortunate not to contract it through work.

. . .

Tom subconsciously felt his throat where his St Christopher used to be. He had forgotten all about it and never expected it to be required. He leant back in his leather office chair and chewed on the end of his pen wondering why she was asking. Curious, he replied, '*Yes – Why? X.*' He sensed by her response that she wasn't being truthful. He didn't know who Dora was, but he was sure that a stranger would not be interested in a photograph of his St Christopher necklace. To buy more time he replied, '*Can't find it atm Laura must have moved it X.*' He hoped that would pacify her for the time being but was doubtful that his message sounded convincing.

Erica was being very persistent, asking if he had lost it. He hated being economical with the truth but he had no option. Trying to flip the situation, he asked her what the big deal was and again was not convinced by her answer. If it was no big deal, why did she even think to ask him about it, he puzzled, absentmindedly biting off the top of his Biro. He angrily chucked the cheap Biro in the wastepaper bin as he attempted to come up with a plan to appease Erica.

Jumping in the car he headed into town. Keynsham has a jewellery shop he thought as he headed to the High Street. It was getting late, so the public car park was not too busy, and he easily found a space. Thankful for the parking app, he paid the requisite sixty pence as he had forgotten to pick up his wallet. He dashed to the High Street and into Pennington's, the Jewellers, hoping that the cost of a St Christopher was not going to cripple him financially. An elderly gentleman, who he assumed to be Mr Pennington, greeted him from behind the old-fashioned counter. In the bright lights of the display cabinet, gold, diamonds, and other precious stones sparkled enticingly.

Conscious that Mr Pennington might be hoping to close the shop shortly, he refrained from idle chatter. Getting straight to the point, he asked to see any St Christopher pendants so that he could choose one for his nephew's eighteenth birthday. Why he invented a cover story was beyond him, but it had felt like the right thing to do in the circumstances. Mr Pennington produced a padded tray with the choice of three designs. One was a rectangular shape, so he discounted it immediately. The other two were circular but two different sizes. It had been so long since he had seen his original one that he struggled to decide which matched it the closest. Finally, he opted for the smaller one of the two. Mr Pennington kindly offered to gift wrap it for him. He had just begun to decline when he thought better of it. It would look odd seeing as it's a gift, he thought, if I refuse. He therefore waited while Mr Pennington painstakingly wrapped the small box and attached a gold bow. He paid the seventy pounds using his phone before stuffing the box into his pocket and heading back to the car. At least this should keep Erica quiet for a bit, he thought as he drove home.

Back in his office, he unwrapped the St Christopher and laid it out in front of him. He took a couple of photos of it but decided to wait until tomorrow to send it to Erica. He had to make it appear as though he had spent a long time searching for it to avoid unnecessary suspicion. Perhaps he should try and tarnish it so that it didn't look so new, he thought, trying to cover his tracks. Putting his face in his hands he lowered his head onto the desk.

He couldn't be sure exactly where he had lost the original St Christopher, but he had a pretty good idea.

Chapter 13

Tuesday 22nd December 2014

Despite turning down Ed and Matt's offer, Tom had not been able to get the thought of teaching Dean Scott a lesson out of his mind since Sunday. What he had done to his little sister was despicable. For all their petty squabbles, he loved Erica and felt protective towards her. While Erica had been asleep, he and his friends had revisited the idea.

Thankfully, Erica was safely back home for the Christmas holidays now, with their parents, who were blissfully unaware of the drama of a few days earlier. Erica had managed to calm down enough to act as if nothing had happened. She was obviously extremely fragile, but he hoped that the break from everything and the festivities would help to clear her head. She had returned to her student accommodation on Monday to pack up for the Christmas break and he was going to join them on Christmas Eve. Laura had gone to visit her family and was due to meet him on Christmas Eve at his parents' home.

. . .

Once Laura and Erica were safely out of the way Tom had called a meeting with Ed and Matt. They had all sat around the table to finalise their plan. Matt had purchased a *'pay as you go'* phone and Tom had acquired Dean's phone number and address from Erica's contacts while she was asleep on Sunday evening. He felt incredibly guilty, but it had been necessary, he convinced himself. Fortunately for Tom on this occasion, Erica was very predictable, so it didn't take much to guess her password. Tom had let out an audible sigh of satisfaction as *Dee-123* lit up the world on Erica's phone. He had quickly scribbled down the information he needed before signing out and returning her phone to the table, leaving her none the wiser.

Now that he had the burner phone, he added Dean's number as the only contact. They began to work out how to lure Dean out of the woodwork to a remote location where they would not be caught on CCTV. Matt contacted their university friend, Jake, who had gone home to Stoke for the Christmas break. They filled him in on Erica's misfortune and their plan to pay Dean a visit. He was keen to help, and they arrange to drive to his home first so he could drive them to a location of their choice. Tom was pleased with this scenario. If there was ever any call for an investigation, they were only visiting a *'uni friend'*. If Jake was picked up on CCTV, he had no obvious connection to Erica or Dean, and it wasn't suspicious for him to be driving in his hometown. They felt like they were getting somewhere. All they had to do now was convince Dean that they were Erica trying to arrange to meet him. The obvious bait was to offer to bring him more money. Erica always referred to him as *'Dee'* and he called her *'Em'*. Tom picked up the phone and began to type, *'This is my new phone, sorry about everything, are you ok?'* He pressed send and they waited. The tension of the moment made them all jump when a reply pinged back.

'Who r u?'

'D Em, I'm worried about u?'

'Plz lend me 300? I'm desperate?'

'Yeh, meet you at yours tomorrow night. I'll txt when there, Em X'

'Cheers x'

They looked at each other, "The fish is on the hook," said Tom as they poured themselves a pre-mission beer.

"We must all wear black with no identifying logos or reflectors, including our footwear," instructed Tom trying to think of everything. "And gloves," he added as an afterthought. He was no criminal mastermind, but he had seen a few real crime programmes and was aware of how to be as unidentifiable as possible. Ed and Matt produced their proposed attire. They had black hoodies, jogging bottoms and brandless black trainers. They had thrown in a black beanie hat to disguise their hair and a neck warmer so that they could cover their faces apart from their eyes. Black gloves completed their look. Ed also had his sunglasses, but the others disappointed him, pointing out that it was going to be dark by the time they carried out their plan. They had a sports holdall in which the baseball bat would be concealed. If anyone saw them, they hoped it would look like they were walking to the sports centre.

They were relying on Jake's knowledge of the area. Tom planned to lure Dee out of his flat on the pretext that *'Erica'* couldn't remember which flat was his. Jake would drop them off in the waste ground behind Dee's flat, so they weren't picked up by any CCTV. There was a high wall that divided the car park from the waste ground designed to obscure the view from the flats. A gap in the wall housed an old garbage bin that would provide cover for the three of them to watch from until Dee was within reach. They would grab him and pull him out of sight of the car park before administering their justice. Once they had meted out their punishment, they had to remember to locate Dee's phone and switch it off. They would then calmly walk across the wasteland to the park, dispose of the phone in the lake and exit into a side road where Jake would pick them up.

On paper it all sounded fool proof, but Tom was starting to feel nervous. Tom was seeing another side to Ed and Matt though, who were keener than ever to '*get the show on the road*'.

They had a couple more beers, recapped their plan and went to bed.

Chapter 14

Wednesday 23rd December 2014

All three were like cats on a hot tin roof when they finally woke up. None of them could settle or eat and they were *'chomping at the bit'* to get going.

"Let's do a last check of our phones before we leave," Tom instructed as it turned 11.30am. "We can put them in the kitchen drawer while we're away."

He hoped that he had thought of everything. If their phones were in his house then no one could trace the three of them to where they were about to go, he thought, feeling pleased with the level of detail and planning.

They were finally on their way. The drive to meet Jake dragged but was uneventful apart from the inevitable road-works. It was 4pm as they arrived, and the sun had set. The night was closing in. There was a biting chill in the air. Tom felt frozen and shivered. The combination of the drop in tempera-ture and his nerves, exacerbated the situation. They hurried inside to the warmth of Jake's home.

. . .

Jake introduced them to his parents who were wrapping gifts in their front room. There was a Christmas tree in the corner and the sound of Noddy Holder reminded them that it was indeed Christmas. They made polite conversation, and it was obvious that Jake's parents were unaware of what they had roped their son into. He was, in essence, their getaway driver. Tom felt a creeping feeling of unease amongst the innocent preparations for the festive season knowing what he and his friends had planned.

Jake brought them all a beer from the kitchen and they adjourned to his room. They quietly finalised their scheme as they drank their beer, hoping for some Dutch courage. It was 8pm when the burner phone pinged with a message from Dee. He was getting impatient and questioning where Erica was. After a quick discussion they agreed to suggest 9pm. Tom sent the text, *'Sorry, delayed, nearly there, see u 9pm, Em X.'*

They said goodbye to Jake's parents and went out on the pretext of going to the pub. Inside the car they donned their beanies, face covers and gloves before crouching low in their seats so that they could not be caught on camera. They arrived far quicker than Tom had hoped. Adrenalin was beginning to pump through his body as Jake pulled up and announced their arrival. "Good luck guys, stay safe, I'll be waiting for you as arranged."

Tom took the lead as the three of them crouched low next to the car park wall and crept towards their hiding place. It was pitch black. There were at least a dozen cars in their nominated spaces. Their windscreens were already frosted solid indicating that they had been parked for some time. A light came on, activated by their movement. Keeping their faces down until they rounded the corner by the bin, they jogged to the relative safety of the waste ground. Once hidden by the wall they gathered their breath and their thoughts. Tom felt his body burning with the adrenalin and was no longer cold. It was only their breath misting in the cold night air that reminded him that it was freezing.

Tom looked around and realised that, in their haste, no one had picked up the holdall with the baseball bat. Just as well, he thought. He was not intending on causing Dee too much damage. He told the others and Ed looked disappointed. "Good job I wasn't relying on it. Thankfully, Matt and I have been researching how best to punch someone," he informed Tom proudly.

Tom took out the phone and was about to send another text when Matt whispered, "How are we going to persuade him to come over here? It's not very plausible that Erica would be hiding from him here!" Tom was annoyed that he'd overlooked such a major detail. It had looked different on the Google map. The only option was going to involve breaking their cover and risk being filmed marching Dee to the waste ground.

Ed spoke up, "We've come this far let's risk it. Two of us can grab him by the arms and the other assist if necessary. Try and make it look like we're his mates meeting him for a smoke or something," he offered, trying to be helpful. "We could hide between the cars. Tell him Erica is waiting in the car, so he'll come looking for her."

. . .

They agreed that Tom and Ed were probably the strongest so should grab his arms and Matt would be back up if required. They waited for the light to go off again before creeping across to hide between two cars. They chose cars that were as far away from the building and as close to the waste ground as possible.

Taking a deep breath, Tom sent the text, *'I'm here, meet me in the car park, can't remember where to go, I'm in my car at the back.'* They held their breath until they heard a door slam closed. From between the cars, they could here footsteps scuffing towards them as Dee came into view. He stopped, apparently looking for Erica's car. The light had come back on due to his movement and they could see him clearly. He had his arms folded, hugging himself to keep warm. He was wearing a hoody, joggers, and a pair of sliders. He obviously wasn't planning to spend too long in the car park, Tom thought, as his target slowly moved towards him. As he approached their hideout, the light switched off again, to the relief of Tom. Their eyes had little time to adjust to the darkness.

Everything seemed to be in slow motion, as Tom and Ed pounced like a cat on a mouse. They each hooked up an arm and frog marched him, with the assistance of Matt from behind, to the privacy of the waste land behind the wall.

Matt squared up to Dee while the others held him. "This is for Erica, you thieving bastard," he growled as he took the wind out Dee with a punch to the Solar Plexus. They had caught Dee completely off guard, and he was now temporarily incapacitated by the blow. Taking advantage of his winding, Ed took the opportunity to express his support of Erica with an upper cut to the jaw. "Try asking for money now," he taunted as he thought he heard a bone crack.

Tom let go of Dee's arm and pushed him to the floor. Sitting astride him he put his hands around his throat as if to throttle him. Dee's arms flailed wildly as he tried to loosen Tom's grip. His hand caught in Tom's gold St Christopher chain that was now swinging over him as Tom lowered his face towards him. "You low life scum bag," he sneered, into his face, "Give one good reason why I shouldn't kill you." Tom pulled his head sharply away from Dee. The adrenalin was numbing, and he did not feel his chain as it was wrenched from his neck. He focussed on the distress in Dee's face which gave him sadistic pleasure. He inflicted an extra squeeze before relaxing his grip. "Lucky for you I'm not prepared to do time," he said, venomously, while deliberately causing Dee's head to bounce on the ground as he released him. Before standing up he retrieved Dee's phone and switched it off. Delivering one last punch to the solar plexus, he stood up stuffing the phone in his pocket.

Tom issued a final warning to the subdued Dee who lay groaning on the floor. "Stay away from Erica," he snarled as something triggered the light in the car park. They could hear footsteps marching towards them. Leaving Dee to lick his wounds they raced across the waste ground to the park. They didn't look back as they reverted to a brisk pace on joining the footpath. Tossing both phones into the lake, they continued to the safety of Jake's vehicle.

. . .

It had felt like hours, but in reality, they had only been out for forty-five minutes. Jake's parents looked surprised when the four of them trooped back in. "The pub was too busy," Jake informed them as they went to his room for a debrief. They looked at each and assessed the damage. Ed and Matt checked their knuckles and were relieved that the gloves had prevented any serious damage. Tom's arms ached from choking Dee and his neck felt sore. He glanced in the mirror and noticed the red mark on his neck. Feeling around, he realised that he was not wearing his St Christopher. He must have lost it in the scuffle, he thought.

They were buzzing from the adrenaline, and no one was feeling tired. They made a solemn vow that no one would ever speak of this again before setting off for home.

Chapter 15

Tuesday 8th August 2023

Erica blindly swiped at her phone to silence the offensive noise, as the alarm roused her from her dreams. It had been a shorter night than she had wished for and 8am had arrived too soon. She and Dora had critiqued various crime shows ranging from Line of Duty to the Death in Paradise spin off, Beyond Paradise. They had both agreed that the latter was a poor representation of rural policing, and the former was a gripping series. Midsomer Murders and a Touch of Frost did not escape their critical discussions regarding plot, authenticity, and acting abilities of the cast. Regardless of any acting ability, they would always watch Grantchester due to the *'eye candy'* that was the vicar. They both agreed that, if the local clergy were anything like Will or his predecessor, Sidney, they would definitely be converted. It was midnight before they finally wound up their reminiscing and staggered back to their respective rooms. Erica couldn't remember how many Malbecs they had consumed but, judging by her head and overwhelming thirst, it must have been at least three large ones.

. . .

She dragged herself into the bathroom where she observed that her tongue was a very dark shade of purple. That will take some work to get shot of, she thought as she grabbed a couple of glasses of water to quench her thirst. Typical when I have a meeting this morning with the man with two names. Two doses of toothpaste and a cup of tea improved the situation. Erica showered and dressed before heading to breakfast. She had a vague recollection that she had agreed with Dora to *do their own thing* so they could have a lie in if they chose and they both had plans for the rest of the day. So much for the lie in, she thought, as she double checked her tongue before dashing to the dining hall for a last-minute breakfast.

She made it by 8.50am and chose to ignore scowls from the catering staff as she grabbed some cereal and toast. Glancing around she noted that some of the committee were also pushing the limits of the breakfast curfew. She therefore confidently plonked herself at a table nearby. She could hear *Brian Blessed* above the crunch of her cornflakes. He was talking about Richard. Her curiosity was aroused. She listened intently as *Brian* sang his praises. Richard was proving his worth as a newcomer to the Summer School in his opinion and he hoped that he would come back for the jubilee in 2024. Evelyn joined in the conversation and Erica had to practically suck the last of her cornflakes in order to overhear what she had to say. Evelyn was obviously aware of Richard's tragic past and smiled sympathetically as she told the others how he had found solace in the new love of his life, Maggie. Maggie was due to be moving in with him when he returned from Swanwick.

. . .

The revelation caused Erica to involuntarily inhale the final drop of milk from her cereal resulting in an undignified cough and splutter session which prevented her from hearing anymore of the conversation. She hoped that nobody had noticed as she attempted to cover up her near-death experience. Disheartened and red in the face, she abandoned her toast, and went in search of a glass of water.

I might have known he would have found someone special by now, she thought as she drifted into the gardens. Finding an empty bench, she sat down to text Lucy and bring her up to speed with the setback of Maggie. As always, Lucy was full of fighting spirit and encouragement despite the setback. '*All's fair in love and war,*' she proffered with a winking emoji. '*He's not dead to us yet! X*'

Erica was not so confident or, for that matter, sure that she should be interested in pursuing anything other than professional guidance from Richard. She played along with Lucy's enthusiasm sending a '*Thumbs up, heart and laughing emoji and X,*' to end the conversation for now.

It was 9.55am as Erica crossed the lawns to the scene of yesterday's awkwardness. As she strolled, she spotted Richard coming from the direction of the main house. His strong tanned legs were visible below his pale blue shorts and his brown leather flip flops '*flipped*' softly as he walked across the grass. She could not help noticing how the short sleeves of his pale pink polo shirt accentuated his bronzed biceps as he gripped his computer bag and the world reflected back from his aviator sunglasses. Erica made it to the table slightly ahead of Richard and daintily took her seat. Richard swung his computer bag onto the picnic table and pushed his glasses up onto his unruly blond locks . A waft of '*Sauvage*' caressed her nostrils as he leant on the table to step over the bench. They were back where they had started less than twenty-four hours earlier.

As Richard unpacked his computer, they exchanged polite greetings. It was all Erica could do to stop herself drooling. There would be nothing more off putting than purple drool she thought recalling the state of her tongue first thing. She watched him arrange his pen and notebook around his MacBook Pro with precision while she worried that he would notice any remnants of her Malbec. She was just instructing herself to not be an idiot when Richard broke the silence.

"I hope you're feeling better this morning?"

"Yes thanks, much better."

"Do you feel like explaining to me what came over you?"

Erica was surprised by the gentleness of his voice which enticed her to offload the whole scenario to him.

"It's all a bit awkward but I'll try."

Erica had expected Richard to be shocked by the revelation that she knew Dean Scott and, more to the point, he was the '*Dick*' in her novel. (She deliberately withheld her suspicions that her brother, Tom, had something to do with his demise. She still wasn't one hundred percent sure and had to give him time to produce his necklace.)

"It doesn't surprise me that the novel you're writing is based on your own experience. I'd guessed that you're '*Stacey*' when I first read your manuscript." His deep blue eyes looked intently at her as he spoke. "It must have been a huge shock to find out that your wish had come true."

"It was. I expected to feel elated instead of sick. It's not what I expected at all. At least it's certain that I'll never get my money back now! I suppose it was meant to give me a feeling of closure if I could dream up a suitable revenge."

"So where does this leave you now? Do you still need my help?" He leaned across and placed his hand lightly on top of her forearm. "I'm happy to help you try and organise your thoughts and plot if you still want to?"

Erica smiled weakly, "That would be very kind if you're sure you haven't had enough of me already?"

"I'll risk one more attempt on one condition."

"What's that?"

"I can understand why you chose it, but would you agree to change HIS name?"

Erica's face fell and she felt the colour rising in her cheeks. She'd forgotten all about the choice of name.

"Oh yes! Of course, I'm so sorry! I hope you're not offended?"

She noticed a broad smile appearing on Richard's face which lit his entire face, as he shook his head.

"Not in the slightest."

Relieved, Erica relaxed and found herself joining in with Richard, who was now laughing.

"What shall we christen him instead?"

Every name that they suggested was rejected by the other due to links with people they already knew and, more importantly, liked. After much discussion they finally named him '*Wayne*'.

"I wonder how real authors choose names for their characters?" She looked at Richard for an answer, but he just shook his head.

"This writing malarky is not as easy as you might think," she stated, sensing his inability to answer her question.

They found themselves talking freely about their love of creative writing. Erica shared her particular love of Shakespeare, the Bronte sisters, and Little Women.

"I suppose I should literally take a few leaves out of their books," she said, recalling some of her favourite quotes.

"'I am not afraid of storms for I am learning to sail my ship'," she continued as Richard listened, intrigued by her quote from Little Women.

"'And so, we beat on, boats against the current, borne back ceaselessly into the past.'"

Erica leant back forgetting she was on a bench, amazed by Richard's response. "F. Scott Fitzgerald, The Great Gatsby," he clarified as she just stopped herself from falling off the bench.

He had thrown down the gauntlet.

"'The only way out of the labyrinth of suffering is to forgive,' Looking for Alaska, John Green." Realising the poignancy of the quote she shot a glance at Richard who seemed unmoved.

"'There is some good in this world, and it's worth fighting for,' JRR Tolkien, The Two Towers." He grinned at her as they competed.

"'Whatever our souls are made of, his and mine are the same,' Wuthering Heights, Emily Bronte." Erica felt embarrassed and hoped that she was not showing it.

Smiling at her, Richard concluded with an air of triumph, "'This above all: To thine own self be true, and it must follow, as the night the day, thou canst not be false to any man,' Hamlet Shakespeare."

They could have carried on with their game, but Richard intervened.

"Shall we stop for a coffee before the crowds arrive?" he asked, glancing at his watch.

Erica nodded and began to pack away. She took it as an instruction rather than a question. It really was down to him what they did as he was doing her a favour by even agreeing to help her. She felt indebted but was feeling more relaxed in his company.

They entered the bar and Richard pointed to the corner, "Why don't you grab those seats and I'll get the drinks."

"Ok, but can I have a tea please?"

"As long as you promise not to throw it at me," he quipped, passing her his computer bag to free up both hands.

Erica navigated her way through the other tables and chairs and collapsed onto the seat. She arranged their bags out of harm's way and waited. It was more comfortable sitting on an upholstered seat and safer with a back to it. She felt cooler indoors rather than sitting in the heat of the sun. Richard came back with their drinks and placed them at, what Erica surmised was, a calculated safe distance. She felt emboldened by his apparent concern for her and surprisingly relaxed since they had laughed together. She was enjoying his occasional teasing. It reminded her of Tom but, thankfully, didn't provoke the same retaliatory response.

"Did you recognise me on the first day when I attacked you with my bag?"

He hesitated before replying with a mischievous glint in his eyes, "Yes. It was a bit of a shock to be honest. But once seen never forgotten Erica. I'm surprised you recognised me though?"

"I didn't. Well, only as Richard Noyles. It was Dora who filled me in, and I nearly fell off my perch! I'd wondered how you appeared to know my name. I thought you must have had good eyesight to read my name badge."

Richard appeared amused as Erica recounted Dora's revelation, but his face became tight as she admitted to her knowledge of Chloe's death. She wanted to remind him of the quote from Looking for Alaska but thought better of it. Instead, she tried to gloss over it and, in an attempt to lighten the mood, changed the subject.

"It was very clever changing your name from Nicholas Ryder to Richard Noyles. I do love an anagram! The only trouble is I don't know which name I should use?"

"Everyone here officially knows me as Richard and I'm kind of getting used to it so perhaps we should stick with that." He paused, before adding with a wink, "As long as you don't shorten it."

"Wouldn't dream of it." she confirmed with a smirk.

The room was filling up with delegates who were grabbing a quick drink before re-joining their respective workshops. The buzz of chatter and laughter reminded Erica that they were in a public space. There was so much more that she wanted to talk to Richard about but was conscious of the lack of privacy in their current surroundings. Richard must have been thinking the same.

"It's getting busy in here and difficult to talk. The weather forecast is fine for this afternoon. I don't suppose you'd fancy going for a walk and we can talk further?" he asked cautiously.

"If you don't have any other plans, that is."

Erica thought she detected a hint of shyness come over him as he made his proposal. After a slight hesitation she nodded in agreement.

"That would be lovely. I could do with the exercise."

"Let's meet after lunch outside the main lecture hall at two," he suggested.

"Lovely, see you then."

Richard retrieved his computer bag before striding off leaving Erica to flop back in her chair to reflect on the morning's developments. She hardly had a chance to think when Dora arrived. "Good of him to warm the seat up for me," she quipped as she landed on the vacant chair. "How's it going?" Dora's eyes sparkled and her mouth dropped as she listened to Erica's summary of the morning thus far.

"Can't turn my back for a second without you throwing something, and now yourself, at Mr Noyles," she joked.

"Before you get carried away Dora, I overheard Evelyn telling the other committee members about Maggie who's moving in with him when he gets home after Swanwick! Apparently, she's the love of his life now."

"Well! he's not behaving as though she is, is he?"

"It's only a walk and a talk we're going on, not a date," Erica corrected Dora. But, in her mind she was just as confused about what she had agreed to. Dora gave a wry smile and tapped the side of her nose with her finger.

"Who knows what Mr Noyles has in mind?"

"Well, I'll find out in a couple hours, won't I?" she countered feigning annoyance. She hoped that Dora would drop the subject and leave her to gather her thoughts.

Dora looked at the clock and, to Erica's relief, made her excuses to leave. "I won't wait up" she laughed as she danced her way through the tables on her way to the next workshop.

Erica closed her eyes to reflect on what had really happened since meeting up with Richard. He had touched her twice now and she hadn't flinched or withdrawn her arm. He had, unexpectedly, made her feel protected and cared for as he had listened and responded to her true-life experience. Was he only empathising with her because of his own tragic relationship, she wondered. Why was he being so nice to her when he must have despised her four years ago at the driving awareness session? Was she mis-interpreting his actions? There were definitely more questions than answers which frustrated her. The most important and biggest question was, where does Maggie fit into all of this?

Erica reminded herself not to lose sight of this huge stumbling block, but her own feelings were making it difficult. Lucy's words, *'All's fair in love and war'*, played on repeat as she wrestled with her emotions. She couldn't deny she was beginning to feel excitement at the thought of their walk and her stomach fluttered in anticipation.

Erica opened her eyes and stood up in preparation to head to lunch. Who am I kidding, she thought as reality kicked in. Why am I allowing myself to begin to dream? It always ends in tears, my tears. Snatching her bag from the floor, she marched to join the lunch queue.

Lunch was a waste of time. Erica had forced herself to down a bread roll with the help of a bowl of tomato soup. Back in her room, she had plenty of time to deliberate over what to wear for her expedition with Richard. She opted for comfort over style and settled on a knee length pair of denim shorts, a white camisole vest top covered with an unbuttoned, light weight, checked shirt. A pair of white trainers finished the outfit. Carla was still confined to barracks, so she took a quick selfie with her before returning her to the dressing table. "Wish me luck," she whispered to the useless, emotionless llama as she glanced at her reflection. She checked for all necessary items. Handbag with phone, key card, credit card and tissues; make up applied and sunglasses perched on her head. All were present and correct as she strode out of her room, down the corridor and out towards the main lecture hall.

Erica checked the time and was relieved that she wasn't late. The area was bustling with candidates who were making their way into the hall for the afternoon session. The time ticked by at a snail's pace, and she was just beginning to feel concerned that she had been stood up when a familiar figure could be seen jogging towards her. He was obviously fit she thought as he arrived in front of her. "Sorry I'm late," he said checking his watch. "Bloody typical that someone chose to phone me just as I was about to leave," he apologised.

"No problem, I've not been here long myself," she lied hoping not to sound too keen. "I hope it wasn't anything bad," she added feebly. She'd really wanted to say, *was it Maggie?* but although her head wanted to know, her heart did not. What she would have done with the information, had she asked, was anyone's guess so she convinced herself she had made the right decision. For now.

"No, just Mum wanting to know how to operate my dishwasher," he replied with a roll of his eyes "She's house and dog sitting." Erica accepted his explanation and smiled. That answered her question about who was looking after Boris, but it didn't eliminate Maggie.

"Why do Mum's have such impeccable timing?"

With a sweeping arm gesture, Richard asked, "Shall we head towards the lake?"

"Why not," said Erica and they set off on the gentle descent to the oasis.

It was a hot, sunny afternoon and the flower beds on the lawn were resplendent and formal. The sunlight accentuated the vivid hues of red, pink, and white Begonias that surrounded either a large pom-pom or pyramid of topiarised green Box. All were encased by low, square Box hedge borders. White planters contained herbs and peach Double Begonias, whilst the herbaceous borders were a mass of variegated Euonymus, large clumps of pampas leaves, topiarised Box and bedding plants contrasted with dark purple Smoke bushes and Berberis.

The blues and purples of the Campanulas, Rosemary and Lavenders provided height and texture, complimenting the reds and yellows of the low growing bedding plants. The Lavender and Rosemary added a sensory experience to the nostrils as the sun warmed their leaves.

. . .

Erica impressed Richard with her knowledge of gardening which she attributed to her mother and grandfather. She impressed herself with how much she could remember. As they made their way down to the lake, they casually shared opinions of their first experience of a Swanwick Summer School. They both agreed that they couldn't have asked for better weather and the setting was perfect for being creative.

"I'll be none the wiser if you make the whole thing up," he laughed as she pointed out some pink Japanese Anemones that were nodding gently in the breeze. "My knowledge only extends to flowers of the bunched variety with a label," he admitted.

When it came to waterside plants, Erica declared that she was *'out of her depth'* to the amusement of Richard. They had begun to circumnavigate the lake. It was blanketed with traditional lily pads with their pink flowers resting regally, like crowns amongst the leaves. Black and gold Karp were nudging the surface and Erica felt as excited as a child at the sight. The surroundings were mirrored in the still clear waters. A Weeping Willow delicately tickled the water's edge producing an occasional ripple to distort the picture perfect image.

Erica whipped out her phone and began to take some arty photos. Richard seized the opportunity, "So what's that stuffed toy of yours all about, if you don't mind me asking?"

Erica blushed as she explained the purpose of Carla the Karma Llama to an intrigued Richard. As she spoke, she scanned his face trying to gauge his reaction to the revelation.

"So, what you're telling me is that it is a therapy toy for the kids and a modern-day class pet?"

"Yes, in a nutshell, she is. It's bizarre how they treat it as if it's real and they're always excited to know what adventure she's had while on holiday or when she's been away at the weekend. It started as a bit of fun one school holiday but now they all fight over who is going to look after her and take her away on adventures. She's been skiing, to the British Museum, up the Eiffel Tower, to concerts and on a yacht. I can't remember everything, but we have photos in the class scrap book. They also have to write a diary of her adventures."

"Sounds bonkers to me. I wish I'd had a crazy teacher like you when I was at school! I would probably have learnt a lot more," said Richard, shaking his head in mock disbelief. "You missed out the Speed Awareness Course," he added with a wink. "I'd like to know what you wrote about THAT in your class scrap book. I must admit, I thought you were a bit crazy when I saw you photographing IT."

Erica was mortified that he had noticed her outside the venue in Bristol. She attempted a laugh, but it was not very convincing. Richard approached a bench and sat down, patting the space next to him. She followed him and sat a respectable distance away afraid of touching him.

"It all makes sense now. I don't know whether you're daft or brave to do all that in public."

He turned to Erica who was fidgeting with embarrassment as he slid closer. "I'm sorry for making you feel uncomfortable. I shouldn't have shown you up in front of the whole group on that day."

"Apology accepted. I think I understand why you were such an arse that day." Richard looked taken aback and slid back the way he had come. "I obviously didn't help by answering you back. But back then, I didn't know it was the anniversary of..."

Richard cut in "I don't think I want to get into this just now. I've apologised and ..."

It was Erica's turn to butt in, "I didn't realise that it's still so painful and I only know what I've read in your book. I obviously don't know you at all or what you're going through. I only remember Nick as the Speed Awareness instructor who was like a bear with a sore head on the day I attended and who showed me up in front of the class. To be honest, I couldn't stand Nick. I can't comprehend that you're the same person. You're a much nicer person than Nick. Hopefully you'll realise that I'm capable of understanding whatever feelings you still have. I just need to know who I'm talking to right now? Richard or Nick?"

"Richard, it has to be Richard. Nick doesn't exist anymore." His voice had reduced to a whisper and Erica was concerned that she had agitated him. This was not what was supposed to be happening.

She found herself sliding closer and put her hand gently on his thigh, "I'm sorry. Please forget everything that I've said. Do you want to call it a day? We can head back if you've had enough."

"No Erica. I'm sorry. I'm angry that I reacted like that. I was enjoying our conversation so let's keep going. Perhaps it would be better if we talked about your novel and not me for a bit."

As one, they stood up and meandered further around the lake.

"I really enjoyed your *'How to get away with murder'* workshop. Perhaps I shouldn't stray too far away from civilisation with you just in case?"

"You're safe – for now!" he grinned. Erica was relieved that he appeared to appreciate her attempt to lighten his mood.

"It's a good job that you still have your St Christopher though or I might have to arrest you on suspicion of murdering 'Wayne, formerly known as Dick'!"

It was Erica's turn to react, "It wasn't me; I wish to God that it was, but it wasn't. I don't know why I feel so awful about it."

They both came to a halt as she turned to look at Richard hoping for an answer. They faced each other and Richard placed one hand on each shoulder as he began to speak softly.

"I'm sorry, that was insensitive of me. We're a right pair! But I guess you've only just learnt of the death of your former boyfriend," he said. "You haven't had time to process the information. Whatever your feelings for him are now, they were, presumably, once good. So, however wronged you have been, it must be hard to totally turn off those original feelings. Your desire for revenge is normal but the reality isn't always as satisfying as we think it will be. The fact it's been taken out of your control and instigated by an unknown person must be confusing and a shock."

Erica was astonished by the perceptive nature of Richard's response. She wrestled against her emotions that were surging through her, threatening to spill forth as floods of tears.

Erica felt warmth and comfort as Richard pulled her close to his chest while the flood gates opened. She closed her eyes and inhaled the now familiar scent of his aftershave as she sobbed gently. Basking in the protection he was offering her with his strong but gentle embrace, she became conscious of the salty damp patch she was creating on his immaculate pink polo shirt. Her makeup was probably rubbing off on him as she blubbed, she thought. Torn between the glorious sensitivity of the moment and the practicalities of his laundry, she peeled her face from his polo shirt, and rummaged in her handbag. She pulled out a handful of tissues and wiped her face before attempting to rescue Richard's polo shirt. Thankfully it appeared damp rather than plastered in foundation. Salt water's good for stains, she thought randomly.

"Oh goodness! You're so understanding. I'm sorry for overreacting. If I've ruined your shirt. I'll replace it. What a state to be in." She felt his guiding arm around her shoulders as they moved to another bench.

"Please don't keep apologising. My shirt's fine, and your reactions are understandable. Let's sit here a moment and just enjoy the peace and quiet."

Erica closed her eyes which heightened her senses. The warmth of the breeze dried the remnants of her tears and cooled her feverish forehead. An orchestra of chirps, buzzing and rustling played in her ears as she tried to soothe her over stimulated mind. Her breathing slowed as she sank into a half-conscious state where she could organise her thoughts and feelings before returning to reality. Reality was dawning all too soon as she wondered what Richard was doing in the quiet of the moment. Without warning, Maggie jumped into her mind. He's probably wishing he was out with Maggie. Why did she have to ruin the moment, she wondered as she half opened her eyes. Richard was looking at her from his end of the bench and smiled softly as she opened her eyes.

"This is wonderful," she smiled cautiously. "Thank you for your patience."

"I'm going to make a suggestion but won't be offended if you don't like it."

Erica nodded her approval.

"Why don't we put your revenge chapters on the back burner and look at the ending that you're wanting to create? If you want to collate some ideas, we could meet up to run through them. It's not my genre but I should be able to assist. I'll give you my number so you can text me when you're ready and we can arrange to meet."

Erica was thinking on her feet. She was still thinking about

Maggie. A guilty feeling swept over her, and she felt adulterous. Hesitantly she replied, "Yes, yes that sounds like a better idea. Are you sure? That's very kind of you. I'll see what I can come up with."

Erica located her phone and tapped in his number to her contacts list. He was safely stored as Richard Noyles. She sent him a '*test*' text message to ensure she had not made an error. His phone pinged to reassure that it was successful.

The sound of approaching voices indicated that it must be at least 5pm. Delegates were pouring out from their various workshops and making the most of the late afternoon sunshine prior to dinner. Erica and Richard looked at each other.

"I suppose we ought to think about heading back," said Erica, as an enthusiastic walker raced along the path.

"Sounds like a plan to me. It's been an interesting afternoon, thank you," he said gently.

"'*And so, we beat on, boats against the current, borne back ceaselessly into the past.*'" he repeated, quoting F. Scott Fitzgerald and The Great Gatsby again, as they began to stroll back to Lakeside. Erica was impressed.

They parted company outside the entrance to Erica's accommodation block. She felt awkward. She didn't know whether to shake his hand, give him a quick hug or a peck on the cheek. Deciding that none of the options were appropriate she raised her hand to give a feeble wave, hoping that it didn't look like a Nazi salute. Richard reciprocated before smiling and strolling off towards the main house.

What the hell was that all about, she thought as she crashed out on her bed?

Erica spotted Dora sitting on a sofa in the foyer of the Lakeside. Dora had waited on the off chance of catching Erica as she walked to dinner. On seeing Erica, she jumped up and linked arms and frog marched her to the dining queue. Erica gave her a brief resume of the afternoon's stroll around the lake which fed Dora's enthusiasm for intrigue and romance.

Erica found herself agreeing to meet Dora at the fancy dress disco at 10pm. The theme was musicals.

"What are you going as? she asked Dora.

"The witch from The Wizard of Oz of course," she replied, stroking her jet-black mane.

"You're not painting your face green, are you?"

"Not sure yet. It depends on how I feel."

"I haven't brought a costume, but I could join you as the scarecrow. *'If I only had a brain'* - I'd only have to look scruffy!"

Dora laughed, unsure if Erica was serious or not.

"I'll see you in the bar. Save me a seat if you get there first. I'm going to spend the evening in my room trying to come up with some ideas for my next meeting with Richard. I've only got tomorrow left to sort this out!"

Erica sat looking at herself in the dressing table mirror. "Who am I kidding?" she said to herself aloud, "I don't have a clue about romance." She looked down at her blank note pad and tapped it with her pen. It was no magic wand, and no words were forthcoming. She filled the kettle and set it to boil. While she waited, she googled *'romance'* hoping that it would inspire her. She wrote down her findings:

Romance – a feeling of excitement and mystery associated with love. The actions and feelings of people who are in love, especially behaviour that is very caring and affectionate.

"That's all very well," she told her reflection, "But, '*I want to know what love is,'*" she sang, trying to do Foreigner's hit single justice. '*In my life there's been heartache and pain, I don't know if I can face it again. Can't stop now, I've travelled so far to change this lonely life.*' She stopped abruptly. The lyrics were too poignant.

In an attempt to kick the song out of her head, she googled '*Love*' and added the definition to her notes.

Love- a quality or feeling of strong or constant affection for and dedication to another. Attraction based on sexual desire: the strong affection and tenderness felt by lovers.

It was clear to Erica that, based on the definitions in front of her, no one had ever loved her in a romantic sense. She, on the other hand, was relieved to confirm that her expectations of love and romance were a perfect match to the definitions before her. Why then, could she not find love and romance? Why was she drawn to a man who already had '*the love of his life,*' Maggie?

Ignoring her own question, Erica tried to focus on what Stacey was going to do. She needed to invent the man who was going to sweep her off her feet. She closed her eyes in an attempt to concentrate but was struggling to deviate from Richard. Opening her eyes, she scribbled a few notes in her notebook before slamming it shut in frustration. Remembering the kettle, she made a hot chocolate. This elicited a sense of indulgence mixed with guilty pleasure as she cupped the mug gently. She focused on savouring the soothing sweetness of the hot velvety chocolate treat. Her phone pinged three times, rousing her from her indulgence. Her stomach flipped at the sight of her first messages from Richard.

'Sorry to interrupt you, are you busy?'

'Just trying to prepare for our next meeting'

'Tomorrow's looking busy and is the last day. Are you free now?'

Erica checked the time. There was still an hour and a half until the disco.

'Can be, what do you want to do?'

'Meet me in reception in twenty minutes and we'll find a quiet spot in Main House'

Erica sent a '*Thumbs up*' emoji and rushed to make herself look presentable.

Erica gazed around the reception area taking it in for the first time since arriving. It was a modernised frontage to the old main house. The magnolia walls looked freshly painted and the curved reception desk was highly polished and looked efficient. Opposite the desk, centrally placed double glass doors opened out to a small glass foyer which subsequently led to the driveway. Inside, sentry duty was being performed by two tall tropical Dragon plants strategically place on either side of the doors. Large bay windows, either side of the entrance, looked out onto the driveway which was decorated with large planters. These contained a cheerful display of red and purple fuchsias contrasted with blue and white lobelias. In each bay window, a two-seater sofa was separated from another by a low coffee table. Erica was about to sit down when Richard appeared. As usual, he sported a smart casual look. He looked fresh in his light beige chinos and a pale blue linen shirt. His tanned ankles could be seen above his brown leather deck shoes which he wore without socks. Erica was relieved that she had changed and felt comfortable in her blue and white floral print tiered midi dress. She loved the flattering V neckline and the floaty cap sleeves helped her feel cool. She was regretting the white denim jacket which felt too warm, but she would probably need it later she thought. She wore her white Converse shoes and carried a small cross shoulder bag.

She took a deep breath as he stood beside her allowing the familiar scent of his freshly applied aftershave to arouse her senses. It was just after 9pm and the sound of delegates increased as they drifted out of the evening talk and began to fill the bar.

"Shall we go somewhere quieter?" Richard asked, looking around. "There's a lounge on the first floor that we could try."

"I'm in your hands, lead on," she replied and followed him across to the stairs. At the top of the stairs was a large glass partition consisting of three arches through which they stepped into the lounge area. Immediately on the left two white arches allowed a view of the corridor beyond. Across each arch was an oak wooden balustrade. A third arch provided access to two corridors, one of which appeared to lead to more conference rooms and another that led to two more bedrooms.

. . .

Erica was in new territory and looked around as they turned right and made their way to a Chesterfield style, dark brown leather settee next to a large window. The old house had high white ceilings that were edged with decorative plaster. To her right were dark wooden bedroom doors recessed in huge white painted arches. The light blue walls and white woodwork reminded Erica of Wedgwood.

"Welcome to my world," said Richard reminding her that his room was located in the vicinity.

"It's wonderful," replied Erica taking in the grandeur. "You even have chandeliers,"

she smiled looking up at the expansive brass light fitting that housed ten candle shaped lamps.

"Oh, how the other half live," she jibed.

"Where to begin?" He looked serious for a moment and Erica began to fear the worst. "I just want to clear the air where Chloe is concerned." Erica tensed, clasping her hands in her lap as he spoke.

"Like you, I'm confused by my feelings of guilt even though our relationship was in tatters already. My counsellor has been over it with me many times but occasionally it resurfaces especially when I am in female company. I know it sounds bad, but I build up barriers when she's mentioned. Believe me, I'm a much better person now than I was four years ago but I don't blame you for hating me when we first met."

Erica waited to be sure that she was not interrupting, "I didn't hate you, I just couldn't stand you at the time. If I'd known what I know now, I would have cut you some slack!"

"I just wanted to apologise for earlier if I made you feel bad for mentioning her to me," he concluded. There was an awkward pause before Erica spoke.

"I'm sorry too for crying all over you earlier. I'm still trying to take it all in. I never expected you to have knowledge of my ex or that he was actually killed. I haven't got feelings for him, but I genuinely would never have wished him dead. Writing this novel is supposed to help me move on but I'm not sure that it is."

"You didn't deserve to get caught up in the world that he lived in. Believe me, those people are master manipulators, and you were very young at the time. You mustn't let it define your life. 'Who controls the past controls the future, who controls the present controls the past'," he said, quoting George Orwell's classic, Nineteen Eighty-Four. "Don't let him control your future."

"I know, but how can I begin to trust anyone again?" She produced her notebook from her bag and opened it to where she had made notes earlier in the evening. She passed it to him. "I had to look up the definitions of love and romance before I could even begin to write about it. I don't stand much chance, do I?"

Erica watched Richard's face which was taut as he read her notes. His eyes became glassy as he appeared to be fighting his emotions.

"Well Erica, you might think YOU don't know what love is but reading this confirms that me and Chloe were definitely NOT in love at the end."

The sound of approaching voices threatened to interrupt their privacy. The DJ was playing the opening song signalling that the fancy dress disco was about to begin. People were making their way to the Vinery and Bar situated below them.

"Do you want to join the fun?" he asked.

"I don't have an outfit, do you?"

"No, it's not really my thing." He hesitated, "I do have some wine stashed in my room if you fancy adjourning there?"

Of course she wanted to, but she didn't want to sound too enthusiastic. She feigned giving it some thought before replying.

"Yes, thanks but I must let Dora know otherwise she'll think I've been kidnapped."

Erica stealthily followed him to his room unsure if fraternising with lecturers was against house rules. Nobody saw them enter through one of the archways, as far as she noticed.

The aroma of freshly sprayed *Sauvage* greeted her as he opened the bedroom door. An abstract artwork, sombrely painted in dark hues, welcomed them. The carpet was a swirly brown and the wall above the wooden headboard of the double bed was papered beige with a striped texture. He had been allocated a large family size room with two beds. It was all very neutral and institutional compared to the teal accents of the Lakeside rooms. The dressing table was only two chairs wide by her calculations, compared to the wall to wall equivalent in her sanctuary. The only chair was more dining than armchair. His laptop and a notebook suggested he used the space as a desk. Car keys and a kindle were the only other items visible as Erica took in the scene. There were no clothes hanging on the chair or tossed on the bed. She visualised all his shirts hanging neatly in the wardrobe indexed by style or colour followed by his trousers and shorts. He appeared to be a meticulously tidy person. A small sash window looked out on the flat roof of the entrance beyond which were some trees, grass, and the carpark. To the right of the window, pushed length ways against the wall, was an unmade single bed. If that had been mine, she thought, it would be covered with all my stuff. She looked around for somewhere tidy to discard her jacket.

She watched on as Richard shut the door before turning to the wardrobe on his left.

"Close your eyes and don't look. If you see where it's hidden, I'll have to kill you," he joked as he retrieved a bottle of red wine. "I hope Malbec is ok. You're not a spy for the SAP squad, are you?"

"What's the SAP Squad?"

"Swanwick Alcohol Police!"

She laughed as she watched him pour the wine into two glasses retrieved from the bathroom.

"Sorry I didn't think to bring wine glasses with me, I hope these'll do?"

"As long as they don't taste of toothpaste, I'm not fussy."

Erica lowered herself onto the single bed, shoving her white jacket out of harm's way. Smiling, she reached to take the glass from him, placing it on the coffee table. Richard confessed to commandeering the table from the lounge when he had arrived. He now wished that he had also *'borrowed'* a small armchair.

Taking out her phone, she sent a text to Dora apologising for standing her up. She omitted any explanation and waited. Dora responded with a sad face and hoped that she was ok. Erica promised to meet her at breakfast before sending a final *'thumbs up and a X'*. She put her phone down on the table and took a sip of wine. Richard was now sitting on the only chair which he had moved nearer to the table. He still had her notebook and was reading through it again.

"So, how are we going to give Stacey a *'happy ever after'* ending?" he asked glancing up from her notes. "What sort of man is she looking for?"

"He needs to be handsome but not vain; strong but not domineering; thoughtful and caring without being a wet blanket or patronising and share her sense of fun, humour and values."

"That's a tall order! Do men like that really exist?" he asked with a smile.

"I don't know, that's my problem! I hope so. That's the beauty of writing. I can invent who I like."

"How can you make it authentic though, if you've never met anyone who fits your specification?"

"I was hoping that you could assist me. You've obviously had more experience than I have of romance." Erica could feel herself at risk of getting tied up in knots. Was he actually fishing? She couldn't tell by his expression, but she thought he might be. Her heart wanted to scream *I've met you, haven't I?* but her head reminded her of Maggie. If there is going to be any connection with him it has got to be instigated by him not me, she asserted to herself. Why am I even interested in a relationship with someone who is prepared to cheat on the *'love of their life'* while away at a conference? Lucy's voice infiltrated her whirring mind playing, *'All's fair in love and war,'* on repeat. She was just convincing herself to go with the flow when Richard sat on the bed, breaking into her thoughts.

"Are you ok love? You look like you're in a trance." He looked concerned as he leaned towards her.

"Oh, I'm so sorry - again- I was just thinking about your question. I think I might have come across someone, but I don't know them well enough." She hoped that she sounded vague enough.

"You can usually tell a lot from first impressions. Maybe you can develop this person as your character, based on what you do know?"

"I'll try, but I've only got one more day left if you're still willing to help me?"

"It may come as a surprise to you Erica, but despite your numerous attempts to attack me and your obvious dislike of me, I am intrigued to help you. My first impressions of you, four years ago, weren't great and I thought I couldn't stand you. With hindsight and what I know now, you were a very funny, if not a little crazy, thoughtful, and caring woman. I actually like you Miss Mills."

Erica was trying not to squirm with embarrassment at Richard's unexpected openness. She reached for her glass to buy some time and savoured the final drop of Malbec. As she reached forward to replace the glass her phone lit up with a notification from Tom. Relief washed over her as she managed to read the first part of the message without picking up the phone. *'Found it,'* was all she could see, but it was enough to finally put her mind at rest that Tom was not responsible for the death of Dean Scott. Days of pent-up worry spilled from her eyes once more in front of an unsuspecting Richard.

Richard was in the process of sharing out the remainder of the bottle of wine as the tears began to drip down her face. "Oh! God, I didn't mean to make you cry again. I was only trying to cheer you up!"

"It's not your words, they were lovely!" She tried to sound reassuring. "I've just had some unexpected, good news."

Richard looked even more puzzled as he moved closer. He had been about to put a comforting arm around her shoulders, but it didn't seem appropriate in light of the tears of joy. Instead, he rushed to the bathroom and reappeared with a toilet roll for her to blow her nose and dry her face.

"I wasn't sure how much you'd need so I've brought the whole thing." He winked, "I thought it would save my shirt!"

Erica was grateful and dabbed at her face trying not to smudge anything. She managed a smile as she pulled herself together and, once again, found herself apologising to poor Richard.

Erica told him about her suspicions and worry regarding the St Christopher that had been found at the scene of Dean's murder. She finally felt able to mention it now that she knew Tom had located his necklace.

"I hope you're not offended that I couldn't confide in you, but I didn't feel that I knew you well enough - and I didn't want to raise any suspicions if there weren't sufficient grounds."

Richard moved closer, reaching his arm around her shoulders, giving her a reassuring squeeze. "I can see now why you reacted earlier when I joked about your St Christopher. The more we're getting to know about us, the better we're going to be at understanding each other."

Erica rested her head on his shoulder, relishing the comforting tone of his voice and the familiar protectiveness of his touch. Her head told her not to read anything into it, but her heart didn't want to listen. She lifted her head, and he removed his arm. She stifled a yawn as the wine and her intense emotions took their toll. Annoyingly, Richard appeared to notice and looked at his watch. "Shall I walk you back to your room, Miss Mills? It's nearly midnight and the disco crowd will be heading off soon. I don't want you turning into a pumpkin on me!"

Reluctantly, Erica grabbed her jacket and stood up. She was relieved to find that the wine hadn't gone to her legs as she picked up her bag in readiness to sneak back to her room. The sound of chatter had diminished but the music indicated that the party was still in full swing. To avoid having to walk through the Vinery, they turned immediately right and rushed past the toilets just as Dorothy dashed into the ladies wearing a gingham dress, white apron and red shoes whilst clutching a wicker basket containing a stuffed toy dog. Turning right they walked through the area housing the coffee machines, which they hoped would be the quieter option before getting to the bar. Passing Hagrid, who was in conversation with Willy Wonka, Elsa, and the Phantom of the Opera, they made their way into the far end of the bar. The shutters were down so there were no characters waiting to be served as they escaped into the concourse which led to the exit.

Erica felt relieved once they were in the gardens. She was feeling flushed and found the evening air refreshing. Clouds were gathering but, the perfect half-moon was still visible. Light from the buildings illuminated the path sufficiently for them as they walked towards the Lakeside. Erica quietly broke the silence.

"Why are we behaving like naughty children?"

"I've got my reputation to think of," he smirked.

"You don't want to be seen with the likes of me then!"

They arrived at the front door and Erica located her key card. It was suddenly very quiet and still as they faced each other to say goodbye.

"Anyway, we haven't done anything naughty," he said, pulling her gently towards him; "Yet."

He bowed his head towards her. Erica surrendered, allowing herself to be drawn to him. Coyly tilting her head upwards to meet him, their lips tentatively touched as he guided her tenderly to him. Erica's whole being fizzed and danced with the promise of more as the intensity increased. The world ground to a halt as they silently communicated their affection in the passion of the moment. It was surreal yet strangely inevitable.

The spell was broken as large drops of rain plopped on the warm path. Erica hurriedly retrieved her key card from her pocket to let them into the foyer. She pulled him playfully through the door.

"That's bad timing," she whispered, exhilarated and breathless from their first kiss. "You might as well wait in my room until it stops. I don't have any alcohol, but I do have hot beverages."

"I have my reputation to think of Miss Mills," he teased again, trying to look reluctant. He allowed her to drag him along the corridor and let him in to her sanctuary.

"This is where this half lives," she announced while scanning quickly for any stray underwear. She was relieved to see that all looked reasonable tidy, for her.

Richard sat on the edge of the bed while Erica made them a coffee. She placed the mugs on the bedside tables and sat with her feet up and back against the headboard. She patted the pillow next to her, "Don't be shy, you can join me if you wish. It's more comfortable than perching on the end." Richard smiled, kicked off his shoes and shuffled up close to her. Once more, they were in each other's arms, letting go of inhibitions, kissing and caressing hungry for more. Erica's emotions were exploding within her.

They could hear the unrelenting rain and it was late.

"You don't have to go if you don't want to," she whispered shyly.

Richard crossed the room and dimmed the lights. Picking up Carla from the dressing table he put her on the windowsill behind the curtains. With a twinkle in his eye, he responded.

"I'd love to stay, if you're sure? As long as Carla's not watching and judging me!"

Chapter 16

Wednesday 9th August 2023

Erica's alarm shattered the silence once more. It was 7.30am and all she wanted to do was roll over to continue dreaming. She hit '*snooze*'. Richard had tried not to wake her as he prepared to creep back to his room. It was 6am and he was hoping not to arouse anyone's curiosity. He had kissed her gently on the forehead which had caused her to stir and pull him to her for one last kiss. He had promised to talk to her later as he dragged himself away.

Now she was pinching herself, struggling to believe that last night had not been a dream. She glanced around and noted that either side of the bed were cups of coffee waiting to be drunk and the other side of her bed smelt of his aftershave. She buried her head into his pillow luxuriating in the memories triggered by his scent. It definitely wasn't a dream, she concluded.

Erica's alarm impatiently reminded her that if she wanted to have breakfast, she really should get a move on. She was at sixes and sevens. Her stomach was doing cartwheels making it impossible to think straight. Deep breathing failed to calm her excitement as she hastily showered and dressed.

She was sitting at her dressing table attempting to apply her makeup when her head finally overruled her heart. *Who am I kidding,* she asked herself, *he will have forgotten me by the weekend when Maggie moves in.* She really needed to talk to Richard. He had promised to catch up with her later and she hoped that she wasn't going to be disappointed.

Feeling anxious, she headed to breakfast hoping to bump into Dora. Poor Dora must be feeling abandoned, she thought as she looked for her in the dining room. She was about to sit down with her toast and tea when Dora grabbed her by the arm, "There you are, you dirty stop out!" she teased before sitting down next to Erica. They had the table to themselves enabling Erica to bring Dora up to speed on yesterday's events. Dora looked fit to burst and giggled like a teenager as Erica admitted that Richard had *'walked her home'* and they had kissed. She erred on the side of *'less is more'* leaving Dora to speculate the rest. "Don't forget to invite me to the wedding, I'm only a few miles from you both." Her whisper sounded like a foghorn to Erica, and she cringed inwardly.

"Sadly, I doubt we'll make it beyond Swanwick," she said lowering her gaze.

Erica shared her concerns about Maggie. Dora looked shocked and disappointed. "How dare he mess you about. You need to talk to him before he breaks your heart. If I wasn't leaving early, I'd give him a piece of my mind. I'm setting off at three so I can be home in time to take Grace to Bristol airport. There's no one to look after Frank if I hang around here."

"I think it's a bit late. I can't stop thinking about him. Why is life always so complicated?"

Dora put a reassuring arm around her, and Erica gave her a tight hug. "Don't forget to keep in touch," Dora instructed. "What's meant to be, will be."

The sun was breaking through as Erica left the dining room, heading for a seat on the lawn. Last night's rain had dried up, but the grass still glistened with dewdrops, waiting for the sun to dull their sparkle. She felt unexpectedly lonely as she crossed the lawn to a vacant bench. Intending to check her social media before texting Lucy with an update, Erica searched her bag for her phone. Even after tipping the entire contents out next to her, she was dismayed. The phone was nowhere to be found.

Erica retraced her steps to the dining room but to no avail. A staff member suggested asking at reception where lost property usually ended up. She trudged through the bar, retracing her steps from the night before. Nobody had handed in her phone, but they took the details in case it turned up later in the day. She sat down in front of the bay window where she had waited for Richard less than twelve hours earlier. Her head was a muddle as she thought first about Richard, then Maggie, and then her phone. She wondered if she had left it in Richard's room, or had he taken it by mistake when he left this morning? Taking some deep breathes and closing her eyes, she attempted to clear her thoughts. She drifted back to Richard leaving and her waking alone. Feeling a complete imbecile, she jumped to her feet and dashed back to her room. It must be in my room. The alarm woke me, and I must have forgotten to pick it up.

. . .

Erica was correct. *'What a state to be in!'* she text to Lucy, filling her in on the *'lost'* phone and her latest quest to find love. Lucy was quick to respond, *'Sounds like U R lovesick! Go girl'*.

Erica confided her concerns about Maggie.

'I told you all is fair in love and war! She's history now he's met you LOL!'.

Erica had predicted Lucy's positivity but was failing to match her outlook. *'How can I find out without making a fool of myself?'*.

'Ask him you idiot!'. Lucy could be straight talking at times, but it was what Erica needed. *'You haven't got all day!'*.

Erica promised to broach the subject with Richard as they signed off with a string of emojis. Hearts, winks, Xs and laughing faces wrapped up their latest conversation.

Erica felt empowered by her friends and resolved to confront Richard about Maggie. She was about to put away her phone when she remembered that she hadn't responded to Tom's text and the picture of his St Christopher. She opened the message and looked at the photo. His message was succinct and to the point, *'Found it, hope Dora likes it! X'*. She took off her own pendant and tried to compare them. As far as she could remember theirs were pretty much identical. As she studied the photo, and zoomed in on it, a feeling of panic came over her. Tom's necklace was different to hers. Texting was no longer an option. She called Tom.

Tom acted surprised to here from her. "Hi Sis, is everything ok?" he asked. Erica didn't know where to begin but tried to get straight to the point.

"I'm worried about your necklace; it doesn't look the same as mine!"

"Why does that worry you? I'm sure they were slightly different. Why are you making such a fuss about them?"

Erica was unable to contain herself any longer, "Dean's dead!" She waited as Tom digested this bombshell.

"What do you mean dead? When? How?" Tom was sounding extremely agitated which worried Erica.

"He was found dead just before Christmas in 2014. He'd been bludgeoned with a baseball bat. They never caught who did it, but they found a gold St Christopher at the scene." She waited again for his response. She could sense that he was pacing up and down as she could hear his breathing getting heavier. He began cursing over and over as he was processing what she had told him.

"What's the matter Tom, you're scaring me!"

"He was alive when we left him, we hardly touched him and definitely not with a baseball bat. I must have lost the chain when we were pulling him about a bit."

"Oh my God Tom, you WERE there. Please swear to me that you didn't kill him."

"Of course I didn't, although I would quite happily have done it. But I wasn't prepared to do time for that low life scum bag."

Tom had no choice but to fill Erica in on his trip to Stoke on Trent with Matt and Ed, on Tuesday 23rd December 2014.

"He was definitely alive and kicking when we were disturbed and legged it," he concluded. "I can't believe that my St Christopher is in an evidence bag belonging to a cold case in a police station in Stoke on Trent," he said in disbelief.

They both promised never to speak of the matter again to anyone before hanging up.

Erica checked the timetable for her last day at Summer School. If she hurried, she could sneak into the first workshop of the morning which promised to unravel the mysteries of writing fiction. She felt guilty that she hadn't devoted as much time as she ought to the various topics on offer. Being preoccupied with her own novel and distracted by Richard was her only excuse. Remembering to pick up her phone, she raced to the popular lecture in the main hall.

The morning flew by as she learnt about developing characters, writing dialogue, choosing strong verbs, viewpoints, introspection, and plenty more. It was a veritable feast of tasty morsels which she devoured enthusiastically. She jotted down notes and spent her tea and lunch break attempting to incorporate her learning into her manuscript. By the end of lunch time, it became apparent to her, she was seriously losing interest in Stacey's quest for revenge and a happy ever after. Her enthusiasm was definitely waning and her desire to become a best-selling author paled into insignificance. She was all consumed by the jeopardy of the relationship between Erica Mills and Richard Noyles.

'I need to talk to you'. Erica looked at the text message, hesitating, unsure if she should send it to Richard. She had hoped to hear

from him by now, but all was silent. She didn't want to appear needy, so she put her phone on the dressing table to give her more time to contemplate. She decided to make a start on her packing to save time in the morning. It was going to be an early check out and she didn't relish getting up any earlier than she had to. Packing her belongings was therapeutic. It was always less stressful packing to leave than to go. All the dirty clothes could be stuffed in one side and all the clean ones stuffed in the other. There was no pressure to avoid creases. She had not bought any souvenirs so she was confident that everything would fit as before.

Erica was seriously considering if she should take a leaf out of Dora's book and just leave early. There were no more sessions that grabbed her. The thought of the AGM and *'Brian's'* booming voice filled her with dread. She had no one to spend the evening with if Richard wasn't interested and, the thought of a singalong around the fire pit reminded her of a short time spent in the Girl Guides. I wonder what *'Ging Gang Goolie'* was all about, she contemplated, stuffing the last few items into her case.

Resigning herself to impending disappointment, she sprawled out on the bed. If she closed her eyes, she could still smell the fading 'notes' of *Sauvage*. Holding his pillow to her and hugging it tightly, she tried not to cry. She wanted to hate him to ease the inevitable pain, but she was hooked. Instead of *reeling HER in*, he was going to throw her back in the water. She could hear Lucy's likely response, *'There's plenty more fish in the sea'*. Dora would just want to *'batter'* him, she thought trying to feel amused at her unintended pun. She wasn't in the mood for jokes, not even her own.

. . .

The previous late night had caught up with Erica and she slipped into a deep sleep. The sound of her ringtone roused her causing confusion as she tried to remember where she was and what she had been doing. Puzzled, she grabbed her phone from the dressing table and took the call. It was Richard. "Hello gorgeous, Hope you've had a good day?"

"Not bad. How about you? I hope you got back safely this morning?"

"Just made it without seeing anyone apart from some mad fool who was out jogging. Anyway, I'm phoning to apologise for not getting in touch sooner. I was desperate to talk to you earlier, but my phone died. I forgot to put it on charge when I got back, crashed out and woke up at nine. I had to dash to my session, and I forgot to pick it up. I haven't had a minute to myself until now as it's the last day. Please forgive me."

He sounded genuine enough to Erica, but she couldn't be sure. She explained her own phone issues before adding, "I'm thinking of leaving this afternoon."

Richard sounded flustered. "But it's nearly six , are you sure you want to leave? I thought we might see each other again?"

Erica was taken aback and glanced at her watch. He was right. She had been asleep for hours. He also sounded concerned.

"Goodness, I'd lost track. Looks like I'll be around for the evening then." Mustering her inner strength she continued, "I'd love to see you. We need to talk. Where and when?"

"I still have some wine in my secret stash if you don't mind coming here?" he offered.

Erica preferred the idea of the privacy of his room and agreed to meet him in the upstairs lounge at 7.30pm.

Erica retrieved a strappy dress from her suitcase and smoothed it out to remove a couple of creases. The sweetheart neckline and fitted bodice complimented her slim figure and the shorter length showed off her toned legs. The feminine white background with pastel florals made her look more tanned than she was. She checked the weather for the evening. It was due to be dry and warm. She decided to dress up her outfit with her flat silver, strappy criss-cross slide-ins and her white denim jacket. She wore her hair half up and ensured that her makeup was understated but flattering. Finally, a squirt of *'J'adore'* completed her preparations. If tonight was the end, she wanted to leave Richard in no doubt about what he was missing out on.

Richard was waiting on the chesterfield sofa as she stepped through the archway onto the landing. He combed his fingers through his blond locks as he rushed to greet her. Her stomach did a triple Salchow once again. He looked as irresistible as ever. His trademark chinos, rolled fashionably at the ankles drew her eyes to his tanned feet that were displayed in his brown leather sliders. His strong chest and arms were accentuated by his pristinely white, slim fit polo shirt. He reached out his arms and gently took both her hands as he bent to peck her on the cheek. "You look stunning," he said as they crept hand in hand to his room.

"So do you," she responded nervously, unsure if that was the right thing to do. She couldn't wait any longer, she needed to know. They stopped in the doorway so he could find his key. As he opened the door she spoke, "I suppose what happens at Swanwick, stays at Swanwick?" she asked.

Richard stopped in his tracks. His face was tense, and he looked serious.

"I hope not. I thought we were just beginning." He paused, appearing to struggle to find the right words.

"But what about Maggie, I heard she was moving in with you when you get back?"

"She is but that won't stop us seeing each other, will it? I'll introduce you to her eventually. She's got the most adorable brown eyes."

Erica gasped and began plotting her escape when Richard closed the door.

"I'm really falling for you Miss Mills and I'd hoped you felt the same?"

"I do but I can't share you with someone else. How can you be so awful?"

Visibly relaxing, Richard tenderly cupped her face in his hands. With a sparkle in his eyes and a broadening smile he looked deeply into her questioning eyes.

"Erica, my darling, I want you in my life more than anything. Because of my work, Boris gets lonely. Maggie is a Golden Retriever rescue dog! I'm collecting her from the RSPCA in Bath on Saturday. You're welcome to come with me if you'd like to meet her? The only thing staying at Swanwick are our bad experiences, and memories of the past."

Erica was struck dumb. She did not know whether to laugh or cry. How could she have been so foolish. She was transfixed by his deep blue eyes as their lips met reassuring them both of the answer.

Chapter 17

Monday 25th December 2023

Erica was still struggling to believe that life was so perfect. It was nine years since she had been duped out of her savings and left with an ingrained distrust of men. She had never dared to believe that she would ever find her *'happy ever after'*. Yet here she was, lying next to the man who had changed everything. It was only four months since they had met but she could not imagine life without him. As he slept next to her, she recalled their coming together in the world beyond Swanwick.

Erica had woken up early as the sun streamed through her bedroom window. She had only been back for a day and was already missing the buzz of Swanwick and the company of Richard and Dora. She had jumped out of bed, wishing she could just nip to breakfast before getting on with the day. Dreamily, she had showered and dressed before resuming her usual routine of making her own tea and toast. She had killed time by sorting through the junk mail that had accumulated in her absence and put a load in the washing machine. She was packing her overnight bag when her phone pinged with a message from Richard.

'Morning Gorgeous, missed you last night, hope you slept well? Boris is looking forward to meeting you! See you at 10am XXXXX.'

Her heart had leapt as she read his text. *'Can't wait! See you soon XXX ,'* she had replied.

She had still been feeling cautious about expressing her true feelings openly. It would take time for her to truly trust that someone as loving and caring as Richard was genuine, but she was trying.

The last night in Swanwick had been magical. They had talked for hours. Erica resolved to abandon her manuscript and Richard finally felt able to forgive himself for Chloe's death. They had eventually fallen asleep in each other's arms. It had been a wrench to say goodbye even though they had agreed to spend the weekend together with Boris and Maggie. Erica had teased Richard that she couldn't possibly stay with two former Conservative Prime Ministers which had caused him to look crestfallen, pleading ignorance to the coincidence. He tried to assure her that he hadn't named either of them. She had shrugged in playful disbelief before kissing him to confirm that she was only joking. Richard had written down his address and they had agreed to meet at 10am on Saturday morning to collect Maggie.

Dora and Lucy were ecstatic when she had told them she was keeping in touch with Richard. They both put themselves forward as chief bridesmaid in presumptuous confidence of the relationship. She had reminded them of her past success rate in the relationship department in an attempt to slow their enthusiasm. Neither of them would back down. They were confident that all would go to plan. Erica eventually succumbed and agreed with each of them that they would feature in any wedding plans should the need arise. Erica had arranged to meet up with Dora in a couple of weeks to keep her in the loop and invited Lucy round for a girl's night in on the Friday night.

Erica had checked the route to the RSPCA Cats and Dogs Home in Claverton Down, on the outskirts of Bath. She had excitedly thrown her walking shoes and bag in the boot of her car before setting off to meet Richard, Boris, and Maggie.

Richard had sprung from his car as Erica pulled up in the car park. The sound of barking filled the air as they embraced warmly. "I've missed you, Miss Mills," he had said as they strolled hand in hand into the reception area to complete the formalities. Half an hour later they returned to Richard's car and Maggie was manoeuvred into the boot. The manager had told them that Maggie was five years old, and her previous owners had split up. Due to their new living arrangements, they were no longer able to keep her. Erica's eyes had welled up as she listened to the story and Richard had hugged her gently. "Sorry," she had said as she wiped her eyes.

"I'm used to it now," he had laughed, kindly.

Erica had followed Richard as they drove to his house which was located between Bath and Bristol. They had unloaded Maggie and introduced her to Boris. They hit it off immediately and there was a cacophony of yaps and wags as they raced around playfully. Richard had shut them in the kitchen so he could show Erica around his Batchelor pad. It was a new build home, and he was yet to decorate. Everywhere was a magnolia blank canvas waiting to be excited with the addition of some colour. He had three bedrooms upstairs, one of which was his office. His bedroom was neat and tidy with a king-size bed flanked by bedside tables. He had a large wardrobe and two chest of drawers. Erica had longed to look inside the wardrobe to see if she was right about him filing his clothes neatly. There was an ensuite as well as a bathroom and both were exceptionally clean. His tidiness and cleanliness had impressed Erica. Richard hesitated at the door of the third bedroom. "I'm not sure if I should show you this room," he had said looking sheepish.

"Up to you," she had responded trying to sound easy going, but her curiosity had been piqued. He had slowly opened the door to reveal another double bed, wardrobe, and chest of drawers. "This is your room," he had teased, so she had slapped him lightly on the arm.

"Fine by me," she had laughed, pushing him out of the door.

Feigning rejection he had slouched out of the room and headed towards the stairs. "I suppose you'll be wanting a tea? Let's see what the PMs are up to in the kitchen."

Erica had floated down the stairs with a bright smile on her face. She already felt comfortable in his home and in his company. She had never been so happy.

Since returning home, they had barely spent a night apart. She was able to commute to her school and he continued to write. She had spent time in her own house when he had to attend writing events, but it felt cold and lonely. She much preferred to be at his and looked after the PMs, as they were collectively known. It was as if they had always been together and were lost when they were apart. Richard always kept in touch regularly and rushed home at the earliest opportunity. Their love of literature was a central part of their life, and they often played the *'quotation game'* that they had started at Swanwick.

She had relished visiting DIY stores and garden centres. It was so much more fun having someone to discuss ideas with even if they didn't always agree. Generally, it was harmonious, and they agreed on most things. Erica was always conscious of the fact it was his house and not hers so didn't feel she had the right to insist on her preferences. He had never implied it once and always insisted on making joint decisions.

There was now some colour on the walls and plants in the garden. There were throws and cushions in the lounge and a spice rack in the kitchen. She had uncovered the truth about the wardrobes. He had admitted that in Swanwick he had shoved all his stuff into the wardrobe to tidy up in case she had agreed to come to his room. At home, it was a bit tidier, but he was not as orderly as she had imagined. She had been allowed to reorganise both bedrooms so that there was room for her clothes in one of the wardrobes. She had been thrilled to learn that he employed a cleaner which accounted for the cleanliness. They had both agreed that there were more important things in life than scrubbing the bathroom and while they could afford it, Shirley was a luxury they were willing to pay for.

Erica had introduced Richard to Tom and Laura who both agreed that he was a billion times better than Dean. They never spoke about the St Christopher necklace, but Erica was convinced that Tom had told her the truth. Laura had given birth to their baby daughter in October, and Erica was now a devoted aunty to Lily May and Tom was a tired, overly anxious father. Even Richard seemed besotted.

Richard finally stirred. "Merry Christmas Gorgeous," he said, as he rolled over to kiss her. "Let's go and see if Santa's been." He was like an excited child as he grabbed Erica's hand and dragged her from the warmth of their bed. They grabbed their dressing gowns and headed to the lounge.

Erica had always dreamt of a Christmas morning with a man that she loved and still could not quite believe that it was really happening. The lights on the Christmas tree fazed in and out and Richard asked *Alexa* to play Christmas music. Beneath the tree, brightly wrapped gifts tempted to be opened. She was mesmerised. Richard left her sitting in the lounge. She drank in the whole experience while he went to the kitchen and poured two glasses of Bucks Fizz. Maggie and Boris wagged their tails furiously as he let them into the lounge. They began sniffing at the gifts sensing that there were some doggie treats waiting to be unwrapped. Richard returned and handed Erica her glass. "Here's a toast to us," he announced raising his glass. Erica tapped his glass with hers, "To us, cheers, I love you." They both sat quietly for a moment and took a sip. With impeccable timing, Alexa was playing Mariah Carey, *'All I want for Christmas Is You'*. Richard pulled Erica to her feet, and they danced around the room, smiling and laughing as they dodged the PMs and the coffee table.

. . .

As Mariah faded out, Richard told *Alexa* to stop. He was still holding Erica's hands as he became serious and addressed her, "'Once upon a time there was a boy who loved a girl, and her laughter was a question he wanted to spend his whole life answering'." He was quoting from The History of Love by Nicole Krauss. He dropped onto one knee and pulled a small box from his pocket which he opened to reveal a diamond solitaire ring. "Erica Mills, I love you so much. Will you marry me?" Erica gazed in amazement as the ring sparkled before her in his outstretched hand. She pulled him back to his feet, and throwing her arms around him, whispered, "Yes. Yes, of course I will. I love you too, Mr Noyles."

As he slid the ring on to her finger, Erica was finally convinced that they were both definitely on the same page.

Printed in Dunstable, United Kingdom

65692533R00088